# CATACLYSM

RYSTAR AND THE LASSOS BOOK THREE

JACK ARCHER

Copyright © 2021 by Jack Archer

Cover and Interior Design by Jack Archer

All rights reserved.

No part of this book may be reproduced in any form or by any electronic or mechanical means, including information storage and retrieval systems, without written permission from the author, except for the use of brief quotations in a book review.

# CONTENTS

| | |
|---|---:|
| Chapter 1<br>*Na'gya Vasilev: Sluirossi, Yimesotwa, Nanyifmil System* | 1 |
| Chapter 2<br>*Rystar Umara: Sluirossi, Yimesotwa* | 15 |
| Chapter 3<br>*Rystar Umara: DSV Firehawk* | 29 |
| Chapter 4<br>*Na'gya Vasilev: Sluirossi, Yimesotwa* | 41 |
| Chapter 5<br>*Rystar Umara: Outskirts of Chure, Yimesotwa* | 53 |
| Chapter 6<br>*Enzo Vida: Tahi Prison, Tahi* | 65 |
| Chapter 7<br>*Rystar Umara: Jeraro Farms, Yimesotwa* | 77 |
| Chapter 8<br>*Rystar Umara: Sluirossi, Yimesotwa* | 89 |
| Chapter 9<br>*Rystar Umara: Yimesotwa* | 103 |
| Chapter 10<br>*Cobalt Torlick: Chure Bubble, Yimesotwa* | 115 |
| Chapter 11<br>*Rystar Umara: Outside Tahi, Nanyifmil System* | 127 |
| Chapter 12<br>*Rystar Umara : DSV Firehawk* | 141 |
| About the Author | 155 |
| Also by Jack Archer | 157 |

# CHAPTER ONE_
NA'GYA VASILEV: SLUIROSSI, YIMESOTWA, NANYIFMIL SYSTEM

Since the death of the *Gloriosum*, Rystar had holed up in her room. Their attacker was still unknown and it set everyone on edge.

It was nice to have Rystar back on the *Firehawk*, even if it did mean she was stomping around the ship, smoking away, and avoiding Kyran as much as she could. They had headed out to Yimesotwa immediately after the battle, hoping no one would follow them.

Na'gya didn't know what to expect on Yimesotwa, but he wasn't ready to meet a group of rogue and possibly hostile Ya'ados. Even if he was the son of Chantakor's Prime Jurat, he was still part of the royalty leading this war on the Ya'ados.

Rystar pestered him with questions, even going so far as to follow him into his room, face buried in her comms tablet, taking notes diligently like any good Tracker Princess. The door shut behind her, and he turned around to raise an eyebrow at her, not getting a response.

"I need to take a shower," Na'gya said pointedly, letting his wings unfurl and stretch in the large room.

Rystar barely looked up, jumping onto his bed and crossing her legs. Na'gya shrugged and stripped his shirt off, followed by his shoes and pants. He wandered to the bathroom and left the door open so he could still hear Rystar, turning on the water and squeezing inside the tiny shower stall.

"Why did you decide to leave Chantakor, anyway?" Rystar called from the bedroom. Na'gya grabbed the soap and lathered up his body, letting the hot water pour over his chest and trying to keep the water away from his wings as best as he could.

"I saw the way the Horoth were beginning to treat us," Na'gya responded, pushing his face in the water spray for a moment, "I didn't want to be a part of it anymore."

"But you were hidden, were you not?" Rystar asked, and he heard footsteps approaching. He turned around to see Rystar leaning against the door and blushed even though she was still looking at her tablet.

"I was hidden the majority of my life," Na'gya sighed and continued to wash, twisting his body in the small space. "I always thought my parents were ashamed of me. Turns out my father was just trying to protect me."

"And your mother?" Rystar's eyes flicked up to him once, then back again to linger. This time, Na'gya did feel a blush creep up his entire body.

"The Jurat?" Na'gya corrected her.

"So impersonal," Rystar chuckled.

"The Jurat is no more my parent than one of the nurses that took care of me when I was little," Na'gya said and turned off the water before holding out a hand to Rystar.

"You don't think the Jurat loved you?" Rystar asked, dragging the towel from its place and handing it to Na'gya. He began to dry himself off and thought about the question for so long that Rystar actually looked up from her tablet. "I didn't mean to suggest—"

"No, you're okay," Na'gya assured her, wrapping the towel around his waist and picking up a brush from the sink to run it through his hair. "I'm sure they loved me in their own way. It just wasn't the way dad loved me."

Rystar held his gaze and seemed to realize for the first time where she was. "I apologize for following you into the bathroom. I'm sure you've had enough of me."

She made to leave, but Na'gya pushed forward and grabbed her hand, pulling her back. They gazed at each other for a moment before a small smile crept onto Rystar's face, and she pulled her hand away to brush some hair from her eyes. "I can be done with questions for now. It's getting late, and I should get going. We've got a big day tomorrow."

"Will you be in your room tonight?" Na'gya asked, wishing he hadn't.

"I might be," Rystar answered, pushing her chin out and clasping her hands behind her back but not moving away from the door. "You planning on visiting later?"

"Not necessarily," Na'gya breathed, stepping closer and watching the color in Rystar's cheeks rise. Sustri were known for their ability to share, but Na'gya had come from a family that mated with one Horoth (or human, in his parents' case) for life. It was hard to quell the jealous fire boiling in his belly, but there was a darker part of him that longed to watch what she and Kyran got up to in their quarters.

"Well," Rystar drawled out, "that's too bad."

"Figured you'd be busy," Na'gya said before

brushing past her and into his room. "If you don't mind, I'll be going to sleep now."

Rystar gave him one last lingering look up and down before crossing the room and exiting. Na'gya followed her and clicked the lock shut, pressing himself against the door and wishing Rystar was between him and it, without clothes and rubbing herself against his unfurling erection.

He let the towel slide to the floor and folded his wings as he laid back on the bed, letting his hand move down to palm himself, sliding a finger into his core. Closing his eyes, he thought of Rystar the morning he'd caught her coming back from Kyran's quarters, hair disheveled and wearing nothing but a tank top and shorts.

He stroked up his tentacle and imagined Rystar's mouth on his skin, kissing down his stomach and hips before sinking down onto him and sucking the life out of him like he knew she could. Na'gya turned his head to the side and brought his free hand up to his mouth to bite down the moans that threatened to escape.

It was the image of Rystar straddling him, bouncing up and down, that sent Na'gya over the edge, and he came while muttering her name into his fist.

The second shower he took that evening was less productive.

---

THE NEXT MORNING THEY ALL STRAPPED THEMSELVES into the chairs on the bridge, looking out of the space shield of the *Firehawk*. The sun glared at them as they headed towards the first border gate, its white-hot insides calling to them.

"Hold on," Lupe muttered and pushed forward on the stick, sending the ship towards the gate and into the familiar tube of time and light. Lupe navigated them expertly through the stars and out of the border gate before pulling up on the stick and sending them towards the second one.

They went through the second gate, emerging on the other side to a magenta sun, twice as big as the one they had seen so far. Na'gya's eyes went wide as he took it in, the enormity of it all, but before he knew it, they were heading towards another border gate, and the sun disappeared.

A small, white dwarf star greeted them in one of the systems. Na'gya hadn't asked which one they were in and, to be fair, didn't exactly care. The engines quieted as Lupe's hands flew over the console and turned them to fly past the sun and towards the blackness of the system.

He couldn't see it but knew they were heading to a small, rocky planet somewhere in the center of the system, and it would take a few hours to get there. Some of the crew began to rise from their seats, and Na'gya followed suit, heading back to the elevator.

The ride to the planet was made in silence. No one knew what to expect from a planet full of Ya'a-dos, especially one so far out in the Bubble. Na'gya wracked his brain for every possible scenario, including the one where none of his brethren cared to see him. That one made him shudder.

Rystar sat with a cup of coffee, her legs folded up underneath her in a dining room chair. Na'gya's stomach was too full of knots to eat.

Enzo was buried in his tablet, swiping away while Cobalt sat in his own chair across from Rystar, his eyes flickering up towards her every so often. Kyran was nowhere to be found, and Na'gya assumed he had stayed on the bridge with Lupe. Shea tossed Na'gya a tired smile before stretching and getting up to visit the coffee maker.

"Nervous?" Rystar asked. The rest of the crew looked up at him, pretending not to be as interested as they were.

"A little," he replied and shifted in his chair, wings stretching out as best as they could in the space.

"I'm sure everything will be okay," Rystar soothed, "we're almost there, and you'll get your answers."

Na'gya nodded, his stomach sinking. Lupe came in on the speakers, their voice echoing through the dining room. "Approaching Yimesotwa now. Will be landing in Sluirossi in about half an hour or so. Get ready."

The weather on Yimesotwa penetrated the ship and chilled them to the bone before they had even landed. Na'gya struggled with a jacket and eventually ripped the back of a large coat into strips to slide over his wings. How he wished there was a store around that sold clothes for Ya'ados.

When they set down, the entire group except for Lupe crammed themselves in the airlock and waited for depressurization before falling out of it and onto the causeway. The port at Sluirossi was far nicer than the ports they had been to on this trip, and they all filed down the metal walkway towards the first checkpoint.

A Sustri guard took their tablets one by one and checked them in, nodding to his brethren in turn before gazing at Na'gya's wings for a moment and taking his tablet. Enzo had programmed a false name into Na'gya's tablet to avoid detection, and so far, it had worked.

"Thank you, Mister Korang," the guard said and nodded, handing Na'gya's tablet back to him. Rystar and Shea went through next with no questions, and Na'gya thanked the port for being so lax with its security. Enzo didn't look too happy about it, even if it put the odds in their favor.

"So, where are we headed?" Kyran turned around when they had made it into the center of the massive foyer, bustling about with all sorts of life forms. Na'gya shifted his weight and scratched an eyebrow. He must have been the only Ya'ados here.

"I'm not sure," he mumbled, looking around as if to see a sign labeled "THIS WAY TO THE RESISTANCE." But there wasn't even another Ya'ados around to follow. "Maybe we can search the communications board for some ideas."

Kyran pursed his lips and took a deep breath, gazing around the foyer and putting his hands on his hips. "Well, we didn't come all this way to look at a damn comms board. Come on, let's get something to eat."

Na'gya blanched and watched as Kyran turned on a heel, heading off towards a plethora of stalls and a giant elevator that disappeared into the ceiling. Rystar shrugged at him and followed, leaving Na'gya in a stunned wake. He shook his head and trotted up after them.

There were so many kiosks and different wares, Qartzl and Sustri, Terran and Atrexean, Horoth, and some he didn't recognize. At one point, Rystar had to pull Shea away from a small shop in the wall that was selling some kind of Terran food Shea hadn't had in years, according to his pleas.

The elevator fit all six of them comfortably, including Na'gya and his pain in the ass wings. He folded them up as best as he could behind him, but they still towered over the rest of them, making him duck even with the tall ceiling.

A quietness settled on the next floor up, a welcome break from the cacophony below. They exited the elevator and turned to their right, following Kyran down a wide walkway lined with native trees. Above them, a curvature of windows showed the howling wind and snow outside.

"Why do you all keep taking us to these shitty planets?" Rystar asked, gazing above them at the horrifying weather.

"Because, sweetheart," Kyran started, glancing back at them, "not every planet can be a winner like Aurum or Yarev. Most of them are tiny rocks fit for nothing but a spaceport."

Try as he might, Na'gya couldn't bristle at the nickname. He shook his head and found himself smiling instead, looking around at all the different stores and wondering if any of them sold clothes that would fit his wings and seeing none. "Where are we going?"

Kyran turned and called back from the front, pointing at a restaurant stuck in the wall in front of them and to the right. "I told you, Prince, we're getting something to eat. Preferably at that hole-in-the-wall, seedy-looking bar there."

Why they were heading to some place like that was beyond Na'gya, but he followed him anyway, blindly, it seemed.

"Six, please." Kyran held up a finger to a bored-looking Sustri server, and they all followed her to a long table near the back of the restaurant. Na'gya slid into the chair near the back to let his wings stretch out. The rest of the group gathered around the table to sit as the server placed menus in front of them and left.

"So, Kyran," Enzo started in that particular *'what the fuck are you doing'* tone he put on so often, "care to tell us why you have the son of the Jurat Prime in broad daylight on a rebel planet?"

"Rebel planet?" Kyran scoffed, ordering them drinks when the server came back. "First of all, keep your god damn voice down. Second of all, the Sustri don't care if the Ya'ados are here. It's the Terrans we need to look out for. I haven't seen any officials, but they could be in plain clothes. That's all the more reason to keep our voices down."

"I'll keep my voice down," Enzo hissed, "but we can't hide those wings."

Subconsciously, Na'gya folded his wings into himself, trying to hide as best as he could.

"Look, you've made him sad," Kyran pouted, taking his drink as the server dropped it in front of him. He took a sip and pointed at the menu, giving his order first. Na'gya ordered some kind of fish and the rest of them placed their orders. He picked up his drink and took a sip, pulling a face at it.

"What the hell is this?" he asked Kyran.

"Charlom," Kyran replied, taking a sip of his own and making a face as well. "Granted, it's Sluirossi's attempt at Charlom, but they're doing their best. Can't fault them, right?"

Na'gya shrugged and took another sip, watching Rystar do the same. "I suppose not."

As they waited for their food, Na'gya looked up and saw someone gliding by the restaurant's windows, someone with a jacket that fit perfectly around the base of their enormous, black, and silver wings. He perked up and watched as the Ya'ados turned into the restaurant and spoke with the server, their hands flying around animatedly.

"Rystar," Na'gya whispered and placed a hand on her arm. She looked down at it before following his gaze to the Ya'ados up front, who was still talking in hushed tones to the server.

"Oh my god," she said, choking a bit on her drink and setting it down. "Kyran, how did you know they'd be here?"

"I didn't," Kyran said and shrugged, red eyes locked on the Ya'ados now, but Na'gya was sure he had brought them here for that reason. Suddenly, the Ya'ados looked up at their table and noticed Na'gya's wings. He pulled a slip of paper from his pocket and handed it to the server, keeping his eyes on Na'gya and nodding.

As he left, Na'gya let go of the breath he hadn't realized he was holding and let his shoulders relax. The server came by the table and set down their food and the slip of paper, presumably from the Ya'ados that had just left. Cobalt, at the end of the table, pushed it to Na'gya and raised his eyebrows at him.

"For you, I believe," he muttered. Na'gya took the paper, flipping it over to see what was written on it.

*6B92-Underground Pass*

Na'gya stared at it for a good moment before handing it to Kyran, who raised an eyebrow at the address before looking back at Na'gya and scoffing.

"These guys sure know how to play, don't they?" Kyran said.

"What's that mean?" Na'gya asked and ignored the fish in front of him. Kyran tucked into a piece of raw meat, fangs bared, and shrugged.

"Underground Pass isn't somewhere I'd go now, much less as first-timers on Sluirossi," he explained. "Although it doesn't surprise me that's where they're holed up."

"Why?" Na'gya asked, taking a bite of fish.

"Full of wonder, ain't you?" Kyran chuckled and took another rip out of his dinner.

"Can't you use your utensils, you animal?" Rystar scoffed and picked up her own fork, possibly to show Kyran what a fork was.

As a response, Kyran picked up his meat and sunk his fangs into it, letting the blood drip down onto the plate below.

"You're awful," Rystar said and shook her head, but Na'gya noticed the dark flush that crept into her cheeks.

They finished their respective meals and paid before downing the last of their drinks and standing up from the table. Kyran led them out, and they stood in a circle out in the walkway, occasionally looking up at the roaring weather above them.

"Underground Pass," Enzo mused, swiping at his tablet and grumbling to himself. "Possibly the worst place we could be right now."

"Or the best place," Kyran said and scuffed at the ground. "Where else would you rather run into a Terran? Here or back on Glasport 2?" He shot a sheepish look at Rystar. "No offense."

"None taken," Rystar grumbled and followed them to the elevators. "Seems like we're not wanted anywhere."

The elevators took them down into a dank and dusty world, full of red lights and steam. Judging by the rocky walls and lack of heating, Na'gya was sure they were underground. He pulled his jacket tighter and followed Kyran down a winding walkway through a throng of Sustri and Atrex scowling at their every move.

Finally, Kyran stopped in front of a stall with the address 6B92 emblazoned in hard metal letters on the front. An old Sustri woman sat behind the counter and plucked at something that looked like a chicken but was most certainly not a chicken. Kyran set an elbow on the counter and raised an eyebrow at her, putting on his most smoldering look. "Hey darlin', what's it going to cost to get back there?"

The woman looked up and huffed, going back to her plucking for a moment before she did a double-take at Na'gya. Gazing at his wings, she nodded at the party and set her not-chicken down on the counter, then beckoned them to join her in disappearing through the door behind her.

Warm air hit Na'gya when he passed through the door, and he sighed, letting his jacket loosen around his body. The old woman shuffled in front of them down winding hallways until they began to see signs of life and more Ya'ados than Na'gya had ever seen.

Rooms branched out on either side of them as they walked, and Na'gya couldn't help but peer into them, noticing Ya'ados with gold wings, silver wings, wings as white as snow, wings as dark as space. He even saw a Ya'ados with bright orange wings that matched his eyes, and Na'gya was startled when he saw his teeth hanging over the bottom of his lip.

*Sustri Ya'ados?*

When they stopped, they found themselves in a large room with a tall, curved ceiling, and the old woman bowed before heading back the way she came. Kyran stood in front of a circular table with a star map laid out on it, and a Ya'ados whose shoulders might not fit through the door.

When he looked up, ice-white eyes met theirs, and a flop of white hair to match was brushed aside as the head Ya'ados regarded them impassively. He wore no shirt, and his skin was purple-black and shone in the low, red light of the room. Snow white wings stretched out on either side of him, larger than Na'gya's.

"I am J'ilan Forswaith, leader of the Wings of

Vengeance," he announced, standing up straight. He must have been almost seven feet tall. "You have three seconds to explain why you're here, or I will have you killed."

Na'gya pushed past his crew to the front and set a hand on Kyran's shoulder to move him aside and present himself. Wings unfurled proudly for the first time in what felt like years, and Na'gya stood tall and unafraid.

"I am Na'gya Vasilev, son of the Jurat Prime and Prince of Chantakor. I am here to give you my aid."

CHAPTER TWO_
RYSTAR UMARA: SLUIROSSI, YIMESOTWA

Na'gya's public declaration of help did not hold nearly as much weight as Rystar thought it would. J'ilan cast his eyes to the Ya'ados around the room and smiled, revealing sharp, white teeth. Rystar blinked.

"You come to us with a group of Terrans," J'ilan began, banging a fist on the table, "the son of the Jurat Prime that seeks to hide any trace of us, and you offer your *aid?*"

J'ilan let out a booming laugh, his wings shaking with the effort of it. The Ya'ados around the room joined in, and Rystar looked at them in turn. There were so many, feathers of all different shades filled the room, and Rystar sunk into the crew, her mind reeling with thoughts of what these Ya'ados could do to them.

"I have risked much to stand before you today," Na'gya continued as if he hadn't heard J'ilan, "I have shunned my family to stand by your side."

J'ilan sobered quicker than his counterparts and snaked around the table to stand in front of Na'gya. He was a statue, angular features etched with rage as his eyes pierced through Na'gya more violently than any sword. "You have the privilege of shunning your parents on your own time. Mine threw me out of the door. A *krokeq*, an abomination, they called me."

J'ilan's eyes whipped around the room at his new family, his new home, and Rystar's heart hurt at the pain in his wild gaze. He focused on Na'gya again, brows furrowed and teeth bared. "They created me!"

A mumble of assent circled the room, and Na'gya froze, chest heaving with the effort of holding back what Rystar assumed were tears. "I'm sorry about your parents, and I'm sorry for the connection I have with those that perpetuate your, our, oppression. But I'm here to fix that."

"Here to fix that, he says," J'ilan hissed, folding his arms in front of him. "Where were you months ago when our people were being slaughtered? Where were you when the Hoop was discovered? What right do you have to come here and insist on aiding us, the Wings of Vengeance?"

"J'ilan, my love."

Another tall Ya'ados, Sustri Ya'ados, by the looks of her teeth, with the same shade of skin but had hair to match, approached J'ilan and rested her hand on his shoulder. J'ilan calmed under her gaze at once, and his eyes lost some of their fire. He hung his head and set his own hand on hers, taking a deep breath before speaking again.

"This is my fiancee, Minabel," he introduced, and she nodded at them in turn. "She is my eyes and ears in this station. While you are here, you will respect her above all others."

Rystar gave the Ya'ados a warm smile which was returned before Minabel let her hand slide down J'ilan's back, tilting her head to look at her fiance. "His right is he is Ya'ados, like us. Too long, we have divided ourselves, especially from our T'ados siblings. The Terran Ya'ados are as much Ya'ados as we. You should know that."

J'ilan grumbled, but his eyes softened when he gazed at her again. With a heavy sigh, he straightened up, puffed out his chest, and held a hand to Na'gya. "Minabel is right, as always. There is too much fighting among us. Please join us for our meal tonight, I'm sure you have many questions, and we have many assignments for you."

"What about the Hoop?" Na'gya asked, taking J'ilan's hand in his own and shaking firmly.

"In time, Heir of Chantakor, in time." J'ilan beckoned them to a door behind them that led to a great hall with several tables and an open kitchen in the back. Many other Ya'ados were mingling around the tables, nursing drinks and throwing furtive glances at them. "Please, help yourself to drinks. Dinner will be served shortly. I must take care of some business before I address the hall."

With a curt nod, he stalked back through the door, leaving them standing awkwardly in the hall as a tight group. Shrugging, Rystar pushed past the throng of their group and sat down at the closest table, bringing her tablet out and beginning to scroll. The rest of the party did the same, with Kyran bringing out his comms tablet and calling Lupe to let him know they weren't dead. Yet.

"So what do you think?" Na'gya asked Rystar under his breath. Rystar didn't move her head but flicked her eyes up to see Na'gya staring directly into her soul.

She cocked an eyebrow, and the corner of her mouth turned up. "About?"

"About all this," Na'gya said, waving a hand

around the hall. "The Wings of Vengeance, all these Ya'ados, the Hoop?"

"Alright," Rystar huffed, clicking her tablet off and setting it on the table. She folded her hands in front of her and sighed so loudly, she got the attention of Kyran and Shea. "What is the damn Hoop?"

Na'gya tilted his head and looked at her before raising his eyebrows and letting out a sigh. "I guess we haven't actually told you what we're doing."

"No, you haven't," Rystar said with wide eyes and a sardonic smile.

"It's hard to explain," Na'gya said, rubbing his face with a hand. "But when I heard about the Ya'ados fighting back through underground channels, I knew I had to come help. I overheard Balee talking about the Hoop to someone one day, and I begged my parents to let me leave on a pilgrimage of sorts."

"Where?" Rystar asked.

"Bufefu," Na'gya replied. "On Ledgorod, one of the only places on the planet where Ya'ados are tolerated. I ran across some interesting things, including a small faction of Ya'ados rebels trying to take back some of their territories. That's when I was captured."

"What happened to the rebels?" Rystar asked, wincing because she knew the answer.

"Capture or killed by a man named Marsters," Na'gya said with a sigh. "We ultimately failed in our mission. And then you found me." He looked up at her and smiled, and Rystar's face flushed again under his gaze. In the middle of a rebel base in a hostile area was the worst time to be having these thoughts, but Rystar was glad she had been sent to Chantakor to save Na'gya.

"And then *someone* ruined my plans," Rystar said, rolling her eyes and throwing a smile at Kyran.

"Don't see you complaining now, sugar," he said, still watching vids.

Rystar hummed, turning back to Na'gya. He was a little less intense now. The fire in his eyes had subsided.

"So tell me about this place," Rystar said to no one in particular, hoping someone would be able to answer her. No one did for a moment until Enzo sighed and spoke up.

"Yimesotwa is a rocky ice world with one continent and a frozen sea," he said, pulling up a map and turning his tablet so she could see. Rystar leaned forward on the table to take it in. "There are three pockets of civilization, all encased in a bubble to keep the weather at bay. Right now, we're in the capital, Sluirossi."

"Why colonize a planet like this?" Shea asked, and Rystar flicked her eyes up to him, happy he was talking again. He had been silent for a while, and she figured she had given him the cold shoulder long enough.

"Seriously, the entire place is frozen over," she agreed, and Shea smiled at her.

"Uranium," Enzo replied, tying up his hair into a bun with a band. "The planet is incredibly rich in it underground. The bubble of Chure is home to some major industrial plants that process it, and there are uranium mines all over the planet."

"Should I even ask who works in them?" Rystar said.

Enzo gave her a wry smile. "Quick to catch on. There wasn't much mining until 20 years ago when the Horoths took over, now it's mostly Ya'ados working in the harsh conditions with little to no pay."

"Why am I not surprised," Rystar said, rolling her

eyes. She was used to humans treating each other like dirt, and it didn't surprise her in the least that alien races treated each other the same way. What she didn't know was the history of the Horoths. Rystar had assumed they were a peaceful race, one that got along with humans.

Dinner was served, and Rystar and Shea were able to pick out something to eat in the spread. There was primarily raw meat and blood wine, but they spotted some of the same noodles Lupe cooked for them, and they grabbed some, heading back to their table with full plates.

"I feel bad leaving Lupe on the ship for so long," Rystar said as she stared into the bowl of noodles.

"They like it there," Kyran said, digging into his meat, whatever it was. "I always invite them to come along on our little adventures, but I think Lupe just likes being alone."

Rystar shrugged, knowing the feeling as she sat among the entire crew, Shea, and Na'gya. Her heart and muscles still ached from the death of the *Gloriosum*, and she was still mad at Kyran for...

*For what, Rystar?*

She shook her head and continued to eat. The foreign vegetables were different from what she was used to but still filling. Food was food, right?

They ate in silence for a while, watching the Ya'ados in the hall mill about, their wings stretched to their full glory. It was amazing, seeing them all in one place, happy to be out of the reaches of oppression, at least for a while.

"Enjoying everything?"

The party looked up to see Ji'lan standing at the head of their table, hands on his hips and nodding at them in turn. "We have an excellent team of Sustri chefs who offered to help feed our group. Even if tensions with the Sustri are high at the moment."

"Are they?" Kyran said with a raised eyebrow, looking around at his crew.

"We believe they have been responsible for some… attacks… on our people," Ji'lan said, clearly not wanting to explain it further. He crossed his arms and eyed their Sustri party with suspicion. "And here, a group of Sustri come with the Heir of Chantakor. I'm eager to learn why you're here."

"And we are eager to tell you," Kyran said, pushing his plate away and standing up to hold out a hand. "Name's Kyran Skylock, Captain of the Mach IV DSV *Firehawk*."

"A LASSO?" Ji'lan said, taking Kyran's hand and narrowing his eyes.

"Stole it from Aurum," Kyran said with a grin, letting his fangs out.

Ji'lan let out a boom of laughter and shook Kyran's hand with more vigor, pulling him in closer and clapping him on the shoulder. "You might just be a friend of ours after all, Mister Skylock."

"We hope to be," Kyran said, letting go of Ji'lan's hand and stepping back. "But we would like some answers. I only kidnapped the Heir of Chantakor to help you folks out, be nice to know what's going on."

Ji'lan rubbed at his stubble with a broad hand and fixed Kyran with a glare before nodding. "I suppose you're right. You've done enough to prove you are on our side. Please, meet me in my quarters back through those doors when you are finished with dinner. I will be waiting."

Kyran touched two fingers to his temple and climbed back onto the bench. "You heard the man, eat up."

Cobalt had opted to bring food back to Lupe on the ship and seemed supremely uninterested in the history of Yimesotwa and the Wings of Vengeance. Rystar, Shea, Kyran, Na'gya, and Enzo all piled in Ji'lan's quarters on various couches and chairs, waiting for Ji'lan to sit in his own seat. The room was large enough for two Ya'ados and their wings and held a kitchen in one corner, a door for the bathroom across from it, and an open space with a gigantic bed for the pair of them.

The walls were a grey brick and covered in maps of Yimesotwa, Bufefu, and other planets Rystar wasn't terribly familiar with. Pictures of cities and bubbles of civilization also covered the walls, their maps littered with strings and lines connecting various places.

"I assume your first question is 'where is the Hoop,'" Ji'lan said, pouring himself a glass of something clear and sitting down in a chair to face them all. Na'gya leaned forward and rested his arms on his knees, clasping his hands together and letting his wings stretch out around him.

"I believe we already know where the Hoop is," he said, tilting his head.

Ji'lan's eyes widened, and he pursed his lips after taking a sip of his drink. "You've spoken with Balee or one of her guard, then."

"Balee," Na'gya affirmed, "on Yarev. They have her imprisoned there."

"I'm aware of Miss Wylo's status," Ji'lan said with a sigh. "She was one of our biggest Terran allies. She had been to the Hoop several times. I can't imagine the things they're doing to her to get that information."

"Whatever they're doing, it isn't working, at least," Na'gya said with a wince, scratching the back of his head. "I haven't heard of any Terrans infiltrating the Hoop so far."

"And why would you?" Ji'lan asked, setting his drink down. "You do not have access to our communications or informants."

"I thought I would have seen a vid on it or something," Na'gya said with a shrug, leaning back in his chair. Rystar admitted to herself that something of the Hoop caliber wouldn't be on any local vids and raised her eyebrows at Shea. She noticed Kyran giving her a side glance but chose to ignore it for now, no matter how bad it made her feel.

"Information about the Hoop is strictly kept to out of band channels only we have access to," Ji'lan explained. "Even the Terran government has not been able to breach our defenses."

"They will eventually," Enzo muttered from his seat, nose deep in his tablet. When no one said anything, he looked up, facing Ji'lan. "Well, your defenses are getting outdated, no offense, and eventually, the Terran government will be able to hack their way in."

"And who are you?" Ji'lan asked, lifting his glass to his lips again.

"Enzo Vida," he replied, *"Firehawk's* security engineer."

"And you think our defenses are outdated?" Ji'lan continued.

"I think they will be very soon," Enzo said. "I think Aurum and the Terran government are constantly working on new ways to infiltrate their enemies and will eventually figure out your defenses, no matter how in-depth they are."

"So what are you suggesting?" Ji'lan said, taking another sip.

Enzo ripped his eyes away from his tablet and set it down in his lap, addressing the entire group now. "When you create your security defenses, you have to make sure you update them every once in a while to keep your attackers on their toes. If you stay stagnant, they'll eventually figure out what your defenses are and how to penetrate them. You're giving them time to figure you out."

Ji'lan nodded, pursing his lips and fixing Enzo with a curious glare. He set his drink down again and stood up, pacing the room with his glorious wings outstretched. "I will admit, we don't have many security engineers on our side to assist us on the cyber front. I would be forever grateful if you offered us your services in that area."

Enzo's eyebrows shot up, and he glanced over to Kyran, who was lounging in his chair, arms behind his head. Kyran shrugged and tilted his head, indicating that it was up to Enzo. Enzo looked back to his tablet and sighed. "I'll assist you as long as I can. Just show me what you have set up so far."

Ji'lan's face lit up with a smile, and he crossed the room to where Enzo sat, holding out his hand. "You have a deal. Come by tomorrow, and I will set you up with Ferrah Akler, our resident network expert."

Enzo nodded again, shaking Ji'lan's hand and becoming buried in his tablet once more. Ji'lan sat back down, and Kyran addressed him this time. "So, boss, we've heard about this Hoop over and over again, and we still don't know what it is. Anything you can do to enlighten us on that front?"

Ji'lan drained his glass and set it back on the table, crossing his legs and setting his hands on his knees. Tapping his foot for a moment, he lapsed into thought before speaking again.

"The Hoop is still a mystery to even us," he explained in a low voice. "From what we've been able to piece together, the Hoop is a base, or a derelict ship, or something of that sort, converted into a secret rebel base that serves as the true rebel headquarters. We receive information from the Hoop every so often, from the *Tachä Chanyem*, the Shadow Band."

"Shadow Band?" Rystar asked as the Sustri's eyes widened.

"We call those on the Hoop the Shadow Band, an old name for those who used secret ways of communicating when the Sustri race was young and at war," Ji'lan explained. "We do not know who the Shadow Band are, though we suspect Balee Wylo was one of them before she was captured."

"The *Tachä Chanyem* have existed for centuries," Kyran said, leaning forward in his chair, brows furrowed. "Do you think these are the same group of folks?"

Ji'lan shrugged. "I have not been around so long as to make that assumption. Several Sustri members of our rebellion began referring to the coded messages from beyond the Bubble as the *Tachä Chanyem* reborn, but I have no stake in these matters."

Kyran hummed, sitting back in his chair and placing his fingers to his lips. Rystar longed to ask him about these things, to learn more about his race and subsequently about him.

"It is getting late, however," Ji'lan announced, standing from his chair. Everyone else took the cue to also stand up, stretching a little before taking Ji'lan's hand in turn. Na'gya was the last and hung back for a moment as the rest of them crowded by the door.

"Thank you for taking us in," Na'gya said, taking Ji'lan's hand again. "I know it must be difficult, taking in strangers, but it means a lot that you trust us. We won't let you down."

"I know you will not, *Wejmo* of Chantakor," Ji'lan said with a smile and held the door open for them to file through.

The walk back to the ship seemed much longer and stranger, having been in a completely different place for a while. The stores around them carried a different weight, and when they reached the top floor, Rystar looked up and out of the ceiling's window. She wondered about the farms and industrial cities Enzo had told them about. Were they really run by Ya'ados slaves? If they were, they had no choice but to stay here on Yimesotwa and free them.

"What's on your mind, darlin'?"

Rystar sighed and turned to face Kyran, watching the rest of the crew hurry ahead to give them ample space to talk without being eavesdropped on. "Please don't tell me we're leaving before we help the Wings of Vengeance free this place."

Kyran fixed her with a soft glare, the red in his eyes more maroon in the dark light of the bubble. "Wouldn't dream of it. This is what our entire goal is, right? Taking care of the Ya'ados and Sustri?"

"I suppose it is," Rystar said, tearing her eyes away from Kyran before her heart betrayed her. "I'm risking my humanity to be here with you all."

"Not all Terrans are bad, you know that," Kyran said, his hand flexing as if he wanted to grab hers. "You heard Ji'lan speak highly of Balee, and she's a Terran."

"She was also part of the Shadow Band," Rystar pointed out. "I'm just… a bounty hunter."

"You're more than that, Rystar," Kyran said softly, and she glanced up at him, confused by the lack of nickname this time. He was silent a moment before clearing his throat and speaking again. "Why don't you come by and see me tonight?"

Rystar's chest burned with desire, how she wanted to stay with him that evening and be with him again. But her head said otherwise and forced her to stick to her guns, whatever they were. "Kyran, I still need time. I don't know what to think yet. I just lost my ship. I need to grieve."

Kyran took in a big breath and looked ahead of him, clasping his hands behind his back and cracking his neck. "You take as much time as you need."

Rystar stopped, and Kyran did too, turning around slightly to face her. She put a hand on her hip and used her other to press two fingers to the side of her head, scrunching her eyes shut.

"It's not that I don't want to, Kyran," she began, opening her eyes and letting her hand fall to her side. Kyran's face lit up for a moment, and he kept silent, listening as she went on. "But, you were in love with my grandfather. I didn't know him, but can't you see why that's a little weird to me?"

"I can," Kyran said quickly, "and I'm sorry I didn't tell you sooner. Out of all the people I could have run into and fallen for, it had to be his granddaughter. You don't think this is weird for me, too?"

Rystar pursed her lips, intent on being angry about that line, but stopped as she processed it. How strange would that be? To live so long, you fall for several members of a family line?

"You said your feelings for me had nothing to do with him," Rystar said, folding her arms across her chest. "Did you mean that?"

"Yes," he replied. She noticed the party far ahead, almost to the space port gates. "I thought it was because of him before I realized that you're your own person. And while the two of you share very similar characteristics, you are also very different."

Rystar glanced up at him through her eyelashes as she faced the ground, almost chastising herself for being upset in the first place. "I'll come to see you later. But just to talk."

"Of course," Kyran said, smiling so wide his fangs dipped below his lip again.

CHAPTER THREE_
RYSTAR UMARA: DSV FIREHAWK

She almost regretted her promise to go see Kyran that evening. Everyone else had gone to bed, and she stood in the kitchen alone, eating an entire sleeve of crackers while sipping on a glass of Charlom. She wasn't drunk, but the delightful tingle of warmth had begun to spread through her body, leaving her with not a care in the world.

First, there was Shea. She hadn't really spoken with him since the FDDS incident and wanted to extend an olive branch. He had been punished enough. Then there was Kyran, the bane of her existence that she refused to fall in love with, who kept pursuing her at every turn.

Enzo took every opportunity to show her the cyber ropes even though she had determined she was worthless when it came to network and security engineering. Still, she enjoyed the moments she spent with Enzo, the way his eyes lit up when she finally understood something he was saying.

Na'gya, his icy blue eyes boring into hers as they spoke, the way he smiled when she was near.

Lupe, who stared at her intensely when they were

cooking, or just whenever. Every moment they could, Lupe would catch Rystar with her favorite food or some other little thing they had found in a shop somewhere.

Cobalt, still an enigma. She had no idea how to open up to the guy, who avoided her whenever he could. Rystar had started to think he didn't like her until Cobalt shoved a fancy new pistol her way when she came back on the ship after the *Gloriosum* exploded. Perhaps he had a soft spot for her, too.

Rystar was so lost in thought, she didn't hear the elevator doors open. The voice that asked for her attention made her look up, and she saw Shea standing there, albeit swaying a little bit.

"What are you doing here?" he asked, heading over to the cabinets to look around. Rystar moved out of the way when he got to the cabinet beside her legs and huffed at him.

"Drinking my sorrows away," she sighed, "what are you doing?"

"About the same," he replied, stopping his searching and hanging his head. She looked down at him and furrowed her brow. "Do you hate me, Rystar?"

He turned his face to her, his deep brown eyes full of guilt, and Rystar most certainly did not hate him. Still mad at him, sure, but definitely not hate. "Of course I don't."

Shea gazed at her for a moment longer before ripping away and continuing to search. "Well, everyone else does."

"You did a bad thing. What do you expect?" Rystar responded, downing the last of her drink and setting the glass on the counter. Shea stopped his rummaging again and pulled out a bottle of clear liquid, closing the cabinet and standing up. He grabbed her empty glass and popped the bottle open, pouring a generous amount of liquid before knocking it back.

"Yeah, I know," he said between his teeth, pouring another and knocking it back, too. Rystar grabbed the bottle from him and set it on the counter, doing the same with the glass, then taking his hands in her own.

"Shea, stop," she said, gazing up at him. He didn't meet her eyes and took a deep breath. "Don't you think I've made mistakes before?"

"Not like this," he said.

"Who cares?" Rystar huffed, pulling him closer. "It's not a competition. You've fucked up, I've fucked up, we're all a huge mess just waiting to be cleaned up. Forgive yourself." She slid a hand up his arm and to his shoulder, guiding it to cup his cheek. "I have."

It took him several moments, but finally, Shea swooped down to catch her lips with his. The taste was something Rystar missed, and she threw her arms around his neck, kissing him deeper. He responded by wrapping his hands around her waist and pulling her closer to him, tilting his head to the side and diving his tongue into her mouth.

They kissed for a while, blissfully aware that everyone on the ship was asleep, and they could do whatever they wanted to each other in this kitchen. She flipped around so that Shea was against the counter and ran her hands down his chest, pushing his jacket to the side. He took the hint and ripped it off, setting it on the counter before his hands were on her waist again, trailing up her sides.

Down she moved until she was nearly kneeling on the floor in front of him, fingers fiddling with the button on his jeans. She opened it and pulled his zipper down, painfully slow, while Shea ran a hand through her hair.

Pulling his jeans down to his mid-thigh, she brushed his boxers aside and grabbed his aching erection as it hit the air. She pumped with one hand while the other cupped his sack, looking up at him through her eyelashes and loving the way his fingers scratched at the back of her head like they couldn't wait for her to be on him.

And soon she was, she licked from the base of his shaft all the way to his tip while he made the most delicious noises at her. She squeezed and sucked his tip into her mouth, letting her tongue swirl around him and chuckling at the way he moaned and grabbed at the back of her hair.

Soon she was pushing him in her throat as far as she could go, the Charlom pushing her along. Her hands pressed against his hips, and he groaned as he sunk his fingers into her hair further and bucked his hips up, sending him further into her mouth. Rystar moaned around him and moved her hands to cup his ass, pulling him into her more.

But the elevator doors dinged again, and she couldn't rip herself away in time to avoid being caught. She whipped her head up and saw Kyran sauntering around the dining table to where they were frozen, the most wicked grin plastered on his face.

"Shame on you for not inviting me to the party..." he drawled, leaning up against the edge of the table and raising an eyebrow. "...Shea."

Rystar blanched and looked up at Shea, who had gone a dark shade of red. She stood up, folding her hands across her chest. "What do you mean?"

Kyran tilted his head at the pair of them. "Well, ever since our little talk, Shea and I came to the agreement that we both wanted to pursue you, and we should make a run at it together."

"Together?" Rystar repeated, turning her attention to Shea. He merely stood there, staring at the ceiling and muttering curses to himself. "What talk?"

"While you were having a little sleep when you came back on board," Kyran started, pushing himself off the table and stepping towards them, "I had the great idea that Shea and I both would treat you to the night of your life. Looks like Shea still wants you all to himself."

Rystar turned to Shea, who had finally brought his head down to look at her. "Is this true?"

Shea closed his eyes for a moment before fixing her with a pleading stare. "I didn't know how to broach the subject. And then tonight, you just came onto me, and I didn't know what to do, I—"

"Easy there," Kyran stopped him, holding out a hand to rest on his shoulder. "Sounds like a classic misunderstanding. After all, how do you broach these subjects with you delicate Terrans?"

"What subject?" Rystar asked slowly.

"About the three of us, sugar," Kyran replied, stepping closer and wiping the corner of Rystar's mouth with a thumb before sucking on it slowly. "I can't imagine you'd be against the idea of it."

Rystar gulped as Kyran's thumb came out of his mouth, slick with spit, and she shuddered, a heat growing low in her belly. She turned to Shea, eyebrow raised. "You're okay with this?"

Shea tapped his fingers on the counter, still fully exposed, and tilted his head at Kyran. If Rystar didn't know any better, she'd say the look she gave him was almost seductive. "I think I'll be more than okay with this."

Kyran's fangs came out again as his smile grew ear to ear, and he flicked his hand at Shea. "Go on and sit back up on that counter so Rystar can finish what she started."

Shea raised his eyebrow but hiked himself up on the counter, taking Rystar's hands and pulling her close again. He was higher now, so she didn't have to sink to her knees to suck him into her mouth. She was bent over, and a pair of hands slid across her back to grab at her hips, and Kyran pressed himself against her ass.

She let out a moan around Shea, and he grabbed at her hair again, pulling her down gently. Kyran's hands snaked up her back, under her shirt, before raking his nails down her back. With Shea in her hair and Kyran groping her thighs and ass, she squirmed in ecstasy, her knees shaking with the effort of keeping her up.

Eventually, her jeans became unbuttoned and slid down her legs all the way to her ankles, where Kyran pushed her feet apart with a boot. She was completely exposed behind him, but it only got her more excited. By the time Kyran had gripped her by the waist and sent two fingers into her core, she was ready and dripping for him.

"God damn, princess," Kyran breathed as he fucked her slowly, pressing his erection against her thigh. She moaned again, mouth busy at the moment, and raised her eyes to watch Shea as he followed Kyran's every movement, mouth slightly open and chest heaving.

Kyran stayed behind her for a while, grabbing every inch of her he could with his free hand, bending down to kiss her hips, and muttering things against her skin. His fangs would drag across her every so often, and she writhed with the sudden pain. She longed for those teeth in her neck and popped off Shea for a moment to catch her breath, pressing her forehead against Shea's stomach and continuing to pump him with her hand.

"I'd say she's pretty much ready for me. What do you think, Shea?" Kyran purred from behind her, and Rystar glanced up at him, her eyes pleading for release, and Shea grinned, pushing against his lip ring with his tongue.

"She's been good, I'll allow it," he said matter-of-factly, but the breathlessness of his voice gave him away. Shea was just as in pieces as she was, and Rystar beamed, sinking back down onto him again, listening to the moans above her.

Kyran's fingers disappeared, and she bucked back, hitting nothing but air as Kyran chuckled darkly. A pair of pants hit the floor. Warm skin pressed between her thighs. Kyran's erection circled her clit, and she had to stop for a moment to catch her breath as he brought her to the brink of orgasm several times, even though he barely moved.

She spread her legs as far as the jeans around her ankles would allow, and Kyran circled her a few more times. Then suddenly, she exploded, her bones catching fire with the sun outside the ship, and she gasped, Shea's hands steadying her shoulders as her legs threatened to give out beneath her.

Panting, she rested her forehead against Shea's thigh as he scratched at her scalp and rubbed her neck. Kyran lined himself up behind her and steadied a hand on the small of her back, the other gripping her thigh and pushed into her core, sighing as he sheathed himself fully. Rystar nuzzled Shea's thigh for a moment as Kyran settled, and she took him into her mouth again, using her hand to grip him by the base and pump slowly with the rhythm her mouth made.

Kyran began to move, sliding in and out of her

easily, and she bucked back against him in time with his thrusts. She planted her hands on either side of Shea's hips and pushed him all the way to the back of her throat, making him cry out and grab the back of her head. He thrust his hips up into her mouth as Kyran picked up his pace, placing both his hands around her waist.

Shea tensed inside her, and she swirled her tongue around him, sucking harder until she felt the familiar release. Pushing him back as far as he would go and swallowing, Shea let out a cry, and Kyran groaned behind her, quickening his pace as Shea released the tension in his muscles and Rystar came up for air, panting hard.

Shea slid off the counter and pulled Rystar close to him, grabbing one of her legs, letting it slip from the jeans, and hooking it under the crook of his arm. He swooped down to kiss her, and Kyran sank his teeth into her neck, pressing their bodies close together as Rystar stood on her toes for Kyran to get a better angle.

She let out a yelp against Shea's lips as Kyran snapped his hips up, letting his fangs out the tiniest bit against her skin.

"More," she moaned between kissing Shea and biting at his lip. Kyran let out a growl and let his fangs sink further into the place where her neck and shoulder met. The pain ripped through her, but the pleasure from Shea's hands cupping her breasts and thumbing her nipples, the way Kyran slid so easily into her at this angle, canceled it out and made her entire body shake.

Shea slid his hand down between Rystar's legs and circled her while Kyran continued thrusting. She came apart again, Shea whispering encouragement against her mouth and Kyran becoming erratic behind her. She pushed against him as he shook with her, placing his sweating forehead against her back and wrapping an arm around her waist.

They all stayed there for a moment, soaking in each other and catching their breath. Kyran pulled away carefully and crossed the kitchen for a clean towel, soaking it in warm water before handing it to Rystar.

"Since I know you're not an entire animal," he chuckled as Rystar swiped it from him and cleaned up. Shea pulled his pants back on, and Kyran did the same, rummaging around in the cabinets for a drink. "Can I pour you two a glass?"

Rystar and Shea nodded their heads, and Rystar sat at the table, pushing some hair from her face and thanking Kyran as he handed her a full glass of Charlom. "I thought just one of you was more than I could handle."

"And now you have two," Kyran said as he sat down next to her, taking a sip of his drink and watching Shea do the same.

Rystar's chest tightened, and she bit her lip. At least Shea and Kyran had worked it out amongst themselves, but she had to tell them both about Na'gya. "Listen, there's something I need to talk to you both about. Well, mainly you, Kyran."

Kyran raised an eyebrow and set his drink down. Shea swirled his glass and stared into its depths, hopefully already aware of what Rystar wanted to talk about.

"I like you both," she began, taking the rest of her glass in one go and sighing at the heat it left down her throat. "And I want to be honest and open with both of you. Even if it means pissing you both off."

"I told you, we talked about this," Shea said.

"I know you did, but talking about it and actually

doing it are two separate things," Rystar pointed out, and Shea pursed his lips. "Kyran, I know you've said the Sustri are fine with having multiple partners, but we humans haven't evolved to that point. Shea, are you sure you can handle this?"

It took him a moment, but Shea took a deep breath and brought his head up to gaze at Rystar. "As long as you still want me, I think I'll be alright."

"I do," she said with a smile, placing her hand over his. Rystar turned to Kyran, who smiled at both of them and downed his drink. "And you, too. But at some point, I'll need to have a conversation with the rest of your crew."

Shea rolled his eyes but chuckled. "I don't know how you're going to manage Kyran and me, much less more than that."

"And I don't know how the Ya'ados feel about multiple partnerships either," Rystar groaned, pinching the bridge of her nose with her free hand. "This is all so confusing. I don't want to hurt any of you."

Kyran put a hand on Rystar's shoulder and rubbed it. "Relax, darlin'. The worst he can do is say 'no,' and I don't think Na'gya's the kind of guy to hold a grudge."

"Speak for yourself," Shea grumbled. Rystar threw him a reassuring smile.

"Give him a little more time," she said, pulling her hand away from his and rubbing her face. "I'd still be upset if I were him, too."

"Yeah," Shea agreed and finished his drink.

"Just go talk to him," Kyran said. "Maybe not right now or in the next couple of days. Let things simmer down, then have a heart-to-heart. He might be more open than you think."

"Hey, Na'gya, I'm already with two guys on the

CATACLYSM

ship. How would you like to be lucky number three?" Rystar practiced, ending her opener with a snort and setting her hand under her chin.

"Maybe practice your proposition a little more, there," Kyran laughed and grabbed their glasses, getting up to rinse them out in the sink. Rystar and Shea stood up, stretched, and headed towards the elevators with Kyran.

"So who are you sleeping with tonight?" Kyran asked as the elevator doors closed. Rystar hit the button that would lead them to the bedroom wing and snorted.

"By my damn self," she said. "You two wore me out."

Kyran let out a bark of a laugh. "If that's all it takes to wear you out, you might want to rethink this six-way relationship of yours."

"Yeah, yeah," she said, waving him off as the elevator doors opened, and she and Shea exited. "Good night."

"Sleep well, you two," Kyran said, and the doors slid shut again.

They stopped outside of Rystar's room, and Shea took both of her hands in his, pulling her close. "You sure you don't want me with you tonight?"

"I wasn't lying," Rystar chuckled, standing up on her toes to kiss him. "Let me have some time to myself."

"Of course," he replied, kissing her back and pushing a strand of hair from her face before pulling away and heading towards his own room. Rystar entered her room and flopped down on the bed, not even bothering to change.

The night's events reeled around in her head, and she bounced back and forth between elation and nervousness. Her stomach was in knots, and she couldn't tell if it was from the fantastic sex or the possibility of being rejected by another crew member. The wind howled in the dark outside. She stared out the window at the swirling snow, icing up the glass and turning her room into a refrigerator.

She bundled some blankets up around her and curled up in bed, falling into a fitful, dreamless sleep.

## CHAPTER FOUR_
NA'GYA VASILEV: SLUIROSSI, YIMESOTWA

Today was the day.

Today was the perfect day to tell Rystar how he felt. Nothing was planned, no excursions, no team meetings, nothing. Na'gya would waltz right out of his room and across the hall to Rystar's, knock on her door, and tell her they should be together, the rest of the crew be damned.

Except Na'gya was stuck behind his own bedroom door, his hand hovering above the handle to open it. His mind was swimming with scenarios, ranging from Rystar declaring her undying love to him to Rystar laughing in his face and jettisoning him out of the airlock.

But Rystar wasn't like that at all. She was kind and understanding. She could get shit done and have everyone follow her happily in the process. Still, it frightened him to even think about the conversation he was about to have with her.

Steeling himself, Na'gya opened the door to an empty hall and left his room, shutting the door and standing in front of it. Rystar's room sat right across from his, and he took a deep breath, gripping the strap to the bag on his shoulder, his feet frozen to the floor. From down the hall, footsteps approached. He turned towards them, watching as Shea made his way down the hallway towards him. When he saw Na'gya, Shea stopped, his eyes going wide.

"Na'gya, how are you?" he asked, taking a careful step closer. Shea was the last person he wanted to speak with right now, much less think about what he was doing with Rystar this early. An icy stab ripped through him as he realized Shea and Rystar were most likely back together at this point, judging from Shea's casual attire and the fact he was down here in the first place.

"I'm fine," Na'gya replied, crossing his arms over his chest and looking away. "What are you doing down here?"

Shea flushed and scratched the back of his head. "Just waking Rystar up for breakfast."

"Is that what you're calling it?" Na'gya said, raising an eyebrow. Shea said nothing but cast his gaze downwards, going silent for a moment before speaking again.

"Listen, I don't think I got the chance to properly apologize," Shea said, taking a big breath and looking back up at Na'gya. "What I did was wrong, and it got your friend killed, and I don't think any apology will be enough to fix that, but I'm sorry anyway."

Na'gya sighed, letting his head fall back a bit as he took in Shea's apology, knowing he meant it, the kid with a heart of gold. It was difficult to process, however. Na'gya could still feel the bits of blood and brain on his skin from where Ju'sif was shot. He shuddered, glancing back at Shea. "I know you were just trying to help Rystar. I would have done the same."

"Really?" Shea asked, his eyes lighting up the tiniest bit.

Na'gya huffed, hating that he could actually forgive the kid for what he did but realizing he meant what he said. "For one of my own, of course."

Shea nodded, gazing back down at his shoes again. They stood there in silence until the door across the hall opened, and their heads whipped up to see Rystar exit her room, wet hair combed back and adorned in fresh clothes.

"Fellas," she greeted cautiously, closing her door with a quiet snap and stepping towards Shea. She stood on her toes to kiss Shea on his cheek, and Na'gya pointedly looked away. "Come on, let's go grab some food before it's gone."

Shea nodded and beckoned for Na'gya to follow them. As Shea and Rystar walked to the elevator, they clasped their hands together, and Na'gya was torn in half.

The kitchen was alight with smells as they got off the elevator and saw the rest of the crew sitting at the table, swiping through their tablets and sipping on their drinks. Lupe cooked in their corner and nodded to the new arrivals.

"About time you joined us," Kyran drawled from the table and put his tablet down, stretching his arms above his head. "You all get enough beauty sleep or what?"

"Hush," Rystar shooshed, swatting at Kyran playfully and sitting down next to him. Na'gya chose the seat furthest away from the throuple and brooded, nodding as Lupe set a cup of some kind of coffee in front of him.

"Listen, *antsuo*, since everyone's here, I need to talk to you about something," Lupe said, taking their spot in the kitchen again, leaning against a counter.

"What's up?" Kyran asked, eyes narrowing.

"Our cards are being declined," Lupe said, raising their eyebrows.

"Impossible," Kyran said, blowing a raspberry.

"I'm sure mine and Shea's are," Rystar mumbled.

"No doubt," Lupe said with a chuckle. "Dead people don't have credits."

"Well, that doesn't make sense," Kyran said, turning to face Lupe. "I have more money than you can shake a stick at. Why the hell is my card being declined?"

Lupe shrugged and spread their hands. "Hell if I know. But I can't buy food or gas, and without those things, we're stuck here."

A collective hush fell around the room as they pondered this new information.

"So what are we going to do?" Shea asked.

"I suppose we could get jobs," Na'gya piped up from the corner.

"Here? In this *sipnäw*?" Kyran scoffed.

"It's better than starving," Rystar pointed out. "And I don't mind earning my keep. I'm sure there's a few bounties we can scrounge up around here. And speaking of dead people, when are going to find out who the hell blew up my ship?"

They all looked around at each other as if they had an answer until finally, Enzo spoke up. "The ship that hit yours wasn't one we've ever seen before. It had brand new technology. I couldn't break into it. Unless they attack again or we find out what it was so I can reverse engineer it, I'm afraid we're at a dead end."

"So that's it?" Rystar said with a smile that did not reach her eyes. Enzo furrowed his brow and gazed down at the table. "Fine. Maybe they'll realize they didn't kill me and come back for more."

Na'gya's tablet dinged, and he pulled it from his bag. The screen lit up with a message from Ji'lan, and he opened it, scanning the words. His eyes widened with terror as he finished and looked up to the crew.

"There's been another bombing," he announced. The reactions ranged from disinterest to horror, and he focused on his tablet again. "They think the Sustris from the Chure Industrial Bubble did it."

"What was bombed?" Rystar asked as Kyran's eyes grew dark.

"The Jeraro Farms, on the north side of the continent," Na'gya said with a gulp.

"They bombed farms?" Kyran piped up. "Why would the Sustris bomb their own farms? This doesn't make any sense."

"Unless they're getting it from the Horoths in charge," Rystar said darkly.

Kyran turned to face her, doubt etched in his face. Na'gya had to admit, on a planet controlled by the Horoths, it might be good to have them on their side. But he was here to liberate them from that, not to blend into the shadows again.

"I refuse to believe the Sustri are helping the Horoths," Kyran said, standing up. "Come on, we're going to speak with Ji'lan now."

Na'gya slid his tablet back into his bag and sighed, throwing a last glance at Rystar before following Kyran out of the room.

---

Lupe and Cobalt had chosen to stay back on the ship as usual. Na'gya followed Kyran through the Sluirossi bubble towards the Underground. Rystar, Shea, and Enzo picked up the rear, and for the first time since his pilgrimage, indeed since the beginning of his adult life, Na'gya felt powerful striding down the walkways with his wings stretched out behind him.

"It's a good look on you," Rystar said, ducking under one of his wings to walk next to him.

"What is?" Na'gya asked, leaning into her without thinking.

"The confidence," she said. "Usually, you have your wings pinned down or something. I can tell you're proud of what you're doing here."

Na'gya smiled, raising his eyes to the ceiling where the blizzard swirled. The sun's light was so weak, it barely penetrated the clouds and turned them into a uniform grey blur against the backdrop of the sky. Snow piled up in the corners of the window panes, and Na'gya shivered, pulling his faded jacket tighter around him.

"I know it's only been a couple of weeks since I was captured," he began, following Kyran into the elevator that would take them to the Underground, "but it seems like a lifetime ago. I can barely remember their faces."

Rystar lapsed into silence as the elevator doors closed and it shuddered around them, descending to their destination. "I think you have more support here and now. We won't let you fail."

Na'gya looked down at her and smiled, watching her green eyes light up with hope, hope that he would be able to accomplish his mission, no matter how hard it became. Taking a deep breath instead of telling her how he felt, Na'gya stepped off the elevator after Kyran and followed him down to the 6B92 building. The old woman showed them to the back again, and they made their way to Ji'lan's quarters.

Na'gya knocked on his door. After a moment, it

opened, Ji'lan's face peering through the crack with suspicion. "I was wondering when you all would show up."

He opened the door fully to let them through, and they filed in, standing around in a circle while Ji'lan shut the door and sat back down in his chair.

"These are the new arrivals?" a voice said from the couch. They turned to see another Ya'ados with pale skin and dark hair and wings sitting forward, arms on his knees and surveying them with narrow, blue eyes.

"Yes, Lo'varth," Ji'lan replied.

"And they are Sustri?" Lo'varth continued, standing up and squaring off with Kyran. Na'gya, upset as he was with Kyran, took a step towards him in solidarity.

"Those two are," Ji'lan said, waving a hand at Kyran and Enzo. They didn't seem bothered by the sudden mistrust, but Enzo brought out his tablet and began pulling up documents all the same, while Kyran puffed out his chest at Lo'varth, despite being the shortest crew member.

"Will you tell us what the hell is going on?" Rystar asked, pulling Kyran back to the center of the group and facing Ji'lan. "You said tensions are high with the Sustri, but you're still working with them."

"Do you know when the *Nukki Tset'ark*, the Wings of Vengeance, was formed?" Ji'lan asked, standing up and crossing the room to place a hand on Lo'varth's shoulder. He settled and Ji'lan continued as Rystar shook her head.

"Two years ago, after the Patros Community Center bombing," Na'gya answered, making Ji'lan turn his head to him with wide eyes. Na'gya returned the glance and shrugged. "I heard about it in the vids.

It was one of the main reasons I went on my pilgrimage to Bufefu."

"I'm impressed," Ji'lan said, turning back to Rystar. "Before the Wings were formed, there were scattered factions of Ya'ados and Sustri all over Yimesotwa, staging coups and little rebellions against the Horoth Government. You see, the Sustri were just as angry at the Horoths as we were."

"Why's that?" Rystar asked.

"Because this was their planet, until about 20 years ago," Ji'lan explained, pushing Lo'varth back onto the couch and sitting back down in his chair. "The Horoths came and, with some fancy government magic, were able to have the planet completely under their rule. Since then, there has been an increase in brutality against the Ya'ados here on Yimesotwa."

"But why would the Sustri's bomb their own cities?" Kyran asked, still glaring at Lo'varth. "Why would they bomb their food supply? It doesn't make sense. The Sustri have always been a friend of the Ya'ados."

"Do not ask me why the Sustri would change sides and begin bombing our community centers, our farms, our manufacturing," Ji'lan said, his voice not raised but dangerous all the same. "Money, power, more food, you name it. There are thousands of reasons to join the dark side."

Kyran said nothing, flipping his head to stare at the ground.

"We still have a few loyal Sustri on our side," Ji'lan went on, the fire in his eyes dying down. "But with the destruction of our farms, I cannot turn a blind eye any longer to the threat they present us. We are fighting two enemies now. Our food is our lifeblood. Without it, they have effectively crippled us."

"It's just the Sustri on Yimesotwa, not all of them," Enzo said, swiping through his tablet. Na'gya craned his neck to see dozens of articles about Sustri support for the Ya'ados back on Glasport 2 and Braluria, their homeworld. "The word is getting out about your struggle, and the Sustri are angry with the Horoth as well. Let us look into this for you. We have the resources."

It was the first time Na'gya had seen Enzo volunteer to help his cause, and it touched him.

"I wouldn't even know where to start," Na'gya admitted, scratching the back of his head.

"Chure," Ji'lan said from his chair.

Na'gya blinked. "Sorry?"

Ji'lan rose from his chair and beckoned for Na'gya to follow him to a large map of Yimesotwa on the wall. The rest of the crew stood behind him, watching closely. Ji'lan pointed to a bubble on the west side of the continent. "This is Chure, the planet's industrial bubble. It is here the Horoth's have the most control."

He moved his finger slightly west of Chure to a large X and tapped on it. "This is where we believe the Horoth's command their troops from. There are many secret goings-on here. If we can leverage a foothold in this base, I believe we will be one large step closer to overthrowing the Horoth hold on Yimesotwa."

"Why haven't you been there before?" Na'gya asked as Ji'lan removed his finger and crossed the room again.

"We have not been able to spare the resources," Ji'lan admitted. "Every time we get close, something or another pops up, and we must divert. I'm hoping you all will be able to assist me with this."

"We can go," Na'gya said with a nod.

"Not all of us," Kyran said, turning to Ji'lan. "I'm going to prove you do have Sustri support at your back."

Ji'lan raised an eyebrow at Kyran, but a grin picked at the corner of his mouth. "And how do you plan on doing that?"

Kyran narrowed his eyes and placed a hand on a hip, tapping his foot and thinking for a moment. "Enzo, are you going with Na'gya?"

"*Oksif*," Enzo replied. Kyran nodded and turned to Shea.

"Shea, you and I are going hunting for the remains of the Sustri government around here, wherever they are," he said before pointing to Rystar. "You can come with me or head out with Na'gya and Enzo, your choice, but I'm sure Na'gya would appreciate the extra firepower."

Rystar nodded and approached Na'gya. "I'll go with you and Enzo."

"I appreciate it," Na'gya said lightly.

The crew began to file out of the room, but Ji'lan stood up and caught Na'gya by the arm before he could leave. "*Nalb*, stay with me for a moment and talk."

"Of course," Na'gya said, waving Rystar away when she turned to look at him. She shut the door, and Na'gya and Ji'lan were plunged into silence except for the tapping coming from the couch from Lo'varth. "What did you want to speak about?"

"I want to know more about you," Ji'lan said, crossing the room to the small cabinets and bringing down a bottle and two glasses. "Being the son of royalty, it intrigues me to know that you left the safe life for something like this."

'Something like this' Na'gya translated to mean 'horrible death sentence,' but chuckled anyway, taking the glass from Ji'lan and smirking. "I felt that I couldn't sit around anymore. The deaths of my brethren were too much for me to bear."

"I heard of the massacre on Bufefu," Ji'lan said, putting the bottle down and taking a sip of his drink. "Was that something you were involved in?"

Na'gya's heart jolted, but he nodded, setting his drink down on the counter. "Yes, me and Ritora. She was the brains, but the Terrans were one step ahead of us."

"Aren't they always?" Ji'lan said with a snort, holding his glass up in solidarity.

"They seem to be," Na'gya agreed, holding his own up and taking a sip.

They sat in silence for a moment, nursing their drinks and becoming lost in their respective thoughts. Finally, Na'gya spoke. "Do you really expect to wrestle Yimesotwa back from the hands of the Horoths?"

Ji'lan said nothing, taking another sip of his drink and looking over at Lo'varth, taking a deep sigh. "I do not expect to take them over so easily. I expect many casualties, many losses. The farms and the industrial side may be easy, but the Horoth have such a strong hold of Sluirossi, even I admit there is no simple way to gain control back."

"And you really think the Sustri are behind the bombings?" Na'gya asked.

"I do not see another scenario," Ji'lan said, sighing and taking another sip of his drink. Na'gya cast his eyes to the maps on the walls, the countless hours Ji'lan put into helping his people and gaining no traction. Na'gya vowed to assist Ji'lan any way he could, even if it meant he had to stay on Yimesotwa for months or even years.

The Hoop could wait.

"We will be ready to infiltrate the Chure base tomorrow," Na'gya said, draining his drink.

"I have faith in you and your crew," Ji'lan said, placing a hand on his shoulder.

"Of course," Na'gya said, setting his empty glass down. He exited the room and headed out into the nearly empty dining hall and through the winding maze. He caught up with the crew near the entrance and waved them on out of the building.

"What did Ji'lan want?" Rystar asked him as they walked down the hallway towards the elevators.

"Just wanted to know a little bit of my background," Na'gya answered. "What I did on Bufefu, what I did before that."

"And what did you do before Bufefu?" Rystar asked.

"Little bit of research," Na'gya replied, remembering his time in the snow and thicket of trees. He missed the simplicity of the time and wished he could go back to it. But he looked down at Rystar, the way she smiled at him with those deep, green eyes, and couldn't for the life of him wish he were anywhere else.

## CHAPTER FIVE_
RYSTAR UMARA: OUTSKIRTS OF CHURE, YIMESOTWA

They had taken the rest of the day to gather their things and create a plan to infiltrate the Chure base just outside of the bubble. Kyran and Shea had taken up residence in the corner of the dining hall, heads together and mumbling to themselves about different factions of Sustri around Sluirossi. Rystar wondered just how close they had gotten.

She, Na'gya, and Enzo had set up shop in the center of the dining room, pouring over maps and trajectories of where they were heading. There did indeed seem to be a base next to the Chure bubble, but it was ten miles away, and in the snow, that would be hell to traverse.

"With our suits, it should be an easy walk," Rystar said, trying to not think about roughly two and a half hours of trudging through possibly the worse blizzard she had ever seen in a bulky snowsuit.

"An easy walk?" Enzo huffed, pulling his hair up into a bun. "There's a reason the cities are in bubbles. We'll need more than just our snowsuits. We'll need our spacesuits on underneath them. Yimesotwa is a Level 1 hazard planet."

"There better be a shitload of uranium on this rock," Rystar muttered, fixing her attention on the map again.

Eventually, they settled on breaking into the side of the base and hooking into the main network to download any information they could from the base. Na'gya stretched greatly and stood up from the table, bidding them good night and heading to the elevators. Soon, Shea and Kyran did the same, and Rystar found herself alone with Enzo at the table.

He swiped through his tablet, seemingly unaware they were alone, and Rystar cleared her throat. Enzo glanced up at her, then around the room. "Where'd everyone go?"

"To bed," Rystar said with a shrug. "I suppose it's getting late."

Enzo hummed, setting his tablet down and stretching, pulling the tie from his hair and letting waves of onyx hair tumble down his shoulders. Rystar sighed and juggled her feelings again, this time landing on Enzo and his burning amber eyes. They looked to her now, and he smiled, something Enzo didn't do very often.

"Feeling okay about tomorrow?" he asked.

"I'm apprehensive," Rystar said, chuckling and setting her arms on the table. she brought out her Cortijet and took a couple of puffs before putting it away and sighing. "Why can't we just break into their network from here, again?"

"It's completely air gapped," Enzo said.

"I thought you said nothing was completely air gapped," Rystar pointed out, narrowing her eyes at him. "And I'm not entirely sure what 'air gapped' means."

Enzo let out a small laugh and yawned before setting his elbows on the table. "A network is usually connected to everything, right? There has to be at least one way out for it to connect to the outside world. Take this ship, for example. It has its own, closed, internal network that talks to everywhere in the ship, and one egress point that allows it to talk to the outside world."

"Okay, I get that," Rystar said, nodding and picturing it in her head. The whole networking and cyber thing never resonated with her. She preferred to just let it do its job and not look into it any further.

"Well, this base has no egress point at all," Enzo continued, raising an eyebrow and letting Rystar consider the implications of that. She frowned.

"So how do they get that information to the outside world?" she asked.

"I assume using physical devices, like our tablets or an external drive," Enzo replied. "They put the information from the base onto their physical device, then deliver it back to wherever it needs to go."

"Seems fussy," Rystar said, crinkling her nose. Enzo laughed and ran a hand through his hair.

"It's incredibly secure," he said, tilting his head and gazing at her. She returned his stare for a moment, wondering where they stood. He was hard to judge, and she found herself going back and forth on whether he was interested in her or not. He took a deep breath and looked down at the table. "So where do you and Shea stand on this whole Kyran thing?"

Rystar's eyebrows shot up into her hair, and she smiled, not wondering anymore. "Shea has welcomed Kyran into the fold. And is open to others. Why?"

Enzo scratched his stubble and flicked his eyes up to Rystar for a moment, a smile playing at his lips.

His foot tapped at the ground, and she grinned back, eager to find out where this was going. "If time permits... we should get a drink when this is over."

"When which part is over?" Rystar asked, leaning forward. "Because this could last a long time, and I'm not a very patient person."

Enzo's grin became wider, and he stood up from the table, Rystar following suit. He walked around to face her and slipped their hands together, bending down, so he was inches from her face. "Well, you'll just have to wait."

The kiss didn't even count as a kiss, more like a brushing of the lips. Rystar sucked in a breath as he moved away and towards the elevators. One last fleeting look, and the elevator doors closed on him, and Rystar slumped into her seat again, resting her chin in her hand.

"Damn everyone on this ship!"

---

WATCHING THE ICE CREEP INTO THE WINDOW PANES made Rystar's bones shiver, but being out there, even with the space and snowsuits, chilled her to the very core.

They eventually decided to not use the Land capabilities of the *Krimson Princess*, opting to go on foot to avoid any surveillance the base might have. Not being able to see more than three feet in front of her brought her mood down even more, but having Na'gya and Enzo next to her warmed her up slightly.

Getting Na'gya into his space and snow suit had been a complete ordeal, complete with Kyran taking out his sewing kit (*"A sewing kit? Really, Kyran?"*) and stitching the rips back up where they had to make room for Na'gya's wings. It was enough to stand out here and not freeze to death, and without further ado, they began to stomp through the snow towards the base.

"According to this map here, we should follow that peak until the base is in sight," Enzo said in their receivers, his voice coming through Rystar's earpiece.

"Can't you just track it on your tablet?" Rystar asked.

"Negative," Enzo said, shaking his head. "It's too cold to keep it out. Plus, they might see the light from the base when we approach."

Rystar pulled a face. They wouldn't be able to see a damn thing in this weather. It took them the better part of three hours to trudge through the snow, occasionally grunting at each other or stopping on a snowdrift to catch their breath. Soon, they saw the dark curvature of a bubble looming in the distance, and they all whooped, heading towards it like it was their salvation.

There were no apparent doors or entry points when they got to it, so they walked around the perimeter, eventually finding a lone door stuck in the wall. They huddled around it, and Enzo brought out his tablet and began to swipe as fast as he could so the encroaching cold wouldn't destroy it.

"Seems like a smart lock," Enzo said over the comms as he swiped this way and that. "Pretty easy to break into, just give me a second."

It was longer than a second, and Rystar's toes were getting more frostbit by the second. She knew better than to hurry him up and bounced on her toes while looking up at the bubble instead. It was certainly much smaller than the Sluirossi bubble. She could see the curvature when she looked to her left and right. But it was still quite large, and she wondered what they were up to in there.

At long last, Enzo exclaimed, and the lock clicked open. Enzo grabbed the door handle and pulled it open, enlisting Rystar and Na'gya's help to push some snow aside for Enzo to squeeze through. One by one, they filed through the door and shut it behind them, finding themselves in near darkness.

The cold pierced their insides here, too, and no one seemed to want to take off their protective gear.

"It's probably better we keep this stuff on, right?" Rystar muttered to them.

"We shouldn't be here long," Enzo said, shaking his head. "I just need to find a jack somewhere to plug my tablet into. Let's check this room over here."

A door sat in the wall down a little ways, and they made their way to it, opening it and pushing themselves inside. Enzo flicked on the light and looked around the room, noticing a wall jack with two openings. He exclaimed in a hushed tone and made his way to it, taking a cord from his pocket and plugging his tablet in.

"Rystar, Na'gya, guard the door," Enzo said, pointing to the door before focusing back on his tablet. "I'm sure they have sensors set up around the place, it won't be long until they find out someone used that door and they send a guard to check it out."

Rystar and Na'gya exited the room and stood on either side of the hallway, with Rystar closer to the outside door. She pulled out a pistol and kept it trained down, her eyes adjusting to the dim light in the hallway. Na'gya stood next to the room Enzo was in, his wings pressed close to his sides.

"Almost done, Enzo?" Rystar asked after a moment. "It's getting creepy out here."

"They're using some new protocol I can't figure

out," Enzo replied, his voice harried. "It's taking me longer than usual to get around it."

"Well, hurry the hell up. I think I heard someone down the hall," Rystar pleaded, taking a deep breath and keeping her eyes on the end of the hall.

"Everyone's in a damn rush," Enzo grumbled.

Several tense moments passed until Rystar and Na'gya jumped at a bang from down the hallway. "Enzo, someone's coming. We have to go."

"Hold them off for a little bit. I'm almost done," came Enzo's voice, and Rystar groaned, not liking the idea of shooting at Horoth government.

A large, dark figure appeared at the end of the hallway and stopped, peering at them as if they were camouflaged in the darkness. They fumbled with something near the waistband of their pants, and Na'gya threw himself into the center of the hallway, stretching his wings as far as they would go.

"Rystar, run," he hissed into the receiver.

"I'm not leaving you both here alone," she shot back, rushing up to him but flying back as Na'gya threw his arm out and pushed her.

"One of us has to make it out of here," he said, standing in front of her as the guard shone his light in the hallway, illuminating the front of Na'gya. He raised an arm to shield his eyes, and Rystar lunged for him again, pulling him out of the way and raising her arm to fire at the guard.

Na'gya ran for the door while Rystar backed away, watching as two more guards came down the hall. She fired. "Enzo, we have to leave, now."

"Two more seconds," Enzo said into the receiver, and Rystar growled as the gun went off in her hand, hitting a guard in the arm. Another pulled out their own gun, and Rystar wasn't stupid enough to have a gunfight in a narrow hallway. More guards rushed at the end of the hallway, and Na'gya opened the door, yelling at Rystar to follow him.

She flicked her eyes to the door of the room Enzo was still in and cursed as she backed away further, and the guards began to swarm it. Turning and heading out of the door, gunshots pinged behind her as they shut it and headed off into the cold.

They listened to the pleas of Enzo as the Horoths stripped him from his gear and the radio went silent. The wind whipped around them, and Rystar would look back every so often to ensure they weren't being followed.

After a while, a couple of snow bikes roared past, and Rystar and Na'gya barreled down into the snow, piling it up around them and waiting until the soft purr of the engines had faded. They walked on again in silence towards what they hoped was the Sluirossi bubble for a couple of hours until the dark curve of it faded into view.

In case the Horoths had alerted Sluirossi to their presence, they circled around, away from the main entrance, to another side door that led straight to the Underground. Rystar pulled out her tablet, shielding it from the cold, and tapped out a message to Shea, asking him to let her in.

When the door opened, Rystar and Na'gya piled through, and Rystar ripped her helmet off. "What the hell was that?"

Na'gya took his helmet off with a little more care and resting it on his hip. "What was what?"

"Sacrificing yourself so I could get out," Rystar said. "Why me, and not Enzo?"

Shea still had the door open and peered out of it as if to see Enzo tromping up the way. Rystar scoffed and waved her hand at him. "You can shut that door. Enzo isn't coming."

Shea shut the door but narrowed his eyes at her. "They caught him?"

"Because white knight here wanted to prioritize me instead of, you know, the guy who has all the god damn answers," Rystar said, her voice raising the slightest bit. Enzo was far more important than her in the grand scheme of things, with his infinite knowledge of the cyber realm and what would have been the Horoths secret base.

Rystar kicked at the ground. Guilt crept into her chest as Na'gya's eyes fell to the floor. It wasn't his fault. It was Enzo's for not listening to them when they asked him to leave. Or it was Rystar's for not unloading into the guards when she had the chance.

Mindreader he was, Na'gya stepped to her and placed a hand on her shoulder. "It's not your fault, I promise."

"I know it's not," Rystar said, her shoulders slumping. "But we still failed, and now we've ruined our chance at getting any information, plus the Horoths will be on high alert now that they know we're onto them."

Na'gya sighed, and Shea walked up to them, motioning for them to follow him down the way and to the Wings' quarters. "Let's warm you guys up and get you something to eat."

"I don't feel like eating," Rystar mumbled, and Na'gya nodded his agreement.

"I don't care. You need to eat," Shea insisted, turning them into a back entrance. "It's been over six hours. You need food."

Rystar stayed grumpy about it but sat down at the table while Shea headed to a table laden with food to grab them both a plate. How convenient, they had made it back just in time for dinner to be served.

When he came back, Shea placed the plates in

front of them and sat down next to Na'gya, across from Rystar. "Kyran will come to see you soon. What are you going to tell him?"

More guilt coursed through Rystar as she thought of Kyran, how disappointed he would be when he found out. "I'm going to tell him the stupid bastard wouldn't listen to me and ended up getting caught."

"He's not going to be happy," Shea said, shaking his head.

"Yeah, no shit," Rystar grumbled, pushing food around on her plate. She sighed and let her fork clatter down as she put her head in her hands. "I'm sorry, Shea. I don't mean to be short with you."

"I understand," Shea said.

After a while of not eating their food, footsteps approached, and Rystar looked up. Kyran made his way to their table and did one sweep before his face fell. "Where's Enzo?"

Rystar sighed. "He got caught, Kyran. The guards rushed us, and he was stuck in a room without us."

"Why'd you leave him alone?" Kyran shot, his red eyes glowing.

"We were watching the hallway," Rystar threw back at him, standing up from her seat to face Kyran. "And I told him to move his ass and follow us, and he didn't."

Kyran took a deep breath and looked like he wanted to punch something but rubbed at his eye and turned away instead. "He's been known to do that."

"Kyran, I'm sorry," Rystar said, stepping towards him and slipping their hands together. "I really tried, but they rushed us so quickly. It was one or all of us."

"You did the right thing, getting Na'gya out of there," Kyran said, turning around to face her, a sad smile on his face. "Who knows what they might have done with Na'gya once they found out who he was."

"We can save Enzo, don't worry," Rystar said.

"Not any time soon."

They looked up to see Ji'lan striding towards them, arms folded across his broad chest and wings flapping behind him. Rystar broke away from Kyran's hands and faced Ji'lan. "I'm sorry, there were just too many guards."

"Do not be sorry," Ji'lan said with a shake of his head. "I sent you in there knowing it was a hopeless case. I only hoped you would get at least some data."

"I wish it were me and not Enzo," Rystar said, "and for that, I apologize."

"I hate to say I agree," Ji'lan said, wincing at his own words. "Enzo's data would have been invaluable to our cause."

Though it was true, it didn't stop the icy stab from ripping through Rystar's chest at Ji'lan's agreement.

"So what now?" Rystar asked, taking in a deep breath and bouncing on her toes, trying not to think about how useless she was in this capacity. "How do we save him?"

"I'm not sure we do just yet," Ji'lan said, picking at a spot on his shirt.

"What are you talking about? We have to go get him immediately," Kyran said, taking a step towards Ji'lan. He looked up, regarding Kyran with an impassive stare.

"He will surely be taken to our moon, Tahi," Ji'lan explained. "It's a low-security prison, and it might be easy for us to make his bail."

"Why would they take someone who broke into their secret base to a low-security prison?" Rystar asked.

"It is low security because our moon has no gravity and no bubble," Ji'lan said with a wry smile. "Escape is nearly impossible."

Rystar growled, sitting down at the edge of the table's bench. "Can we at least try?"

"They will most certainly identify your LASSOs and keep you from entering," Ji'lan said, scratching his chin. "And we have no ships for you to use. I am at a loss of ideas for your friend."

Rystar put a hand over her mouth and rested her elbow on her knee, looking up at Kyran, who merely stood there with his hands on his hips. A hush fell over the crew, and they remained in the hall for a long time.

## CHAPTER SIX_
ENZO VIDA: TAHI PRISON, TAHI

On the one hand, he couldn't believe Rystar and Na'gya would just leave without him. On the other, he did have a habit of saying "two more minutes" when they really didn't have two more minutes.

The Horoths had stripped him of his gear, and he felt terribly naked as they gripped him under the arms and dragged him to a cell somewhere far away from where they caught him.

Part of Enzo was furious they had left him behind, but when he saw just how many guards had swarmed the hallway, it made sense to him. No use in them all getting caught and hung out to dry.

They tossed him into the small cell, and he stood up to gather his bearings when the door clanged shut. Dim light filtered through the bars and shone down on a lone cot with no blanket and a bucket Enzo shuddered at. No window adorned the wall and Enzo's heart sank. Even though there was nothing but snow outside, he still liked having the ability to stare out at the blur of grey and white.

Enzo had tossed and turned on his tiny cot, only

moving when the guards brought him a sliver of food stacked haphazardly on a tray. His face itched with a three-day-old beard, and his hair hung in clumps around his chin. No part of his body or clothing was clean. He laid on his back on the cot, unmoving, for many hours at a time. It must have been days before a Horoth guard came to yank him out of the cell, slap a pair of handcuffs on him, and push him roughly down the hallway.

The ride to Tahi went smoothly, as smooth as a prison ride could be, and after a few hours, they docked at the Tahi prison. Enzo was shoved off board and led off the ship and into an airlock that transformed into an old, worn building.

The hallways went on and on, twisting and turning, and Enzo lost count of all the doors they pushed through. They passed other cells with prisoners, rooms holding massive computers that spanned from the floor to the ceiling. Enzo found himself craning his neck to take a look despite his situation.

An office loomed into view. As they approached it, the hard grip on Enzo's arm became tighter as they opened the door and flung him inside.

"Chief Brosond," the Horoth guard greeted. "This is the man we found breaking in several days ago."

"And you're just now bringing him to me?" the Chief drawled, pushing his glasses up his nose and raising his head to regard his office's new intruders.

"There's been a backlog of prisoners, sir," the guard replied.

"But this one has a very interesting tablet," the Chief said, holding up Enzo's tablet. Enzo's heart hammered in his throat. Even though he had set his tablet to encrypt its sensitive files upon capture, anything could be broken into.

"My apologies, sir," the guard said, bowing his head.

"Leave us," Chief Brosond sighed, waving the guard away and motioning for Enzo to sit. Enzo sat in the worn chair and put his handcuffed hands between his knees. The guard shut the door, and they sat in silence for a few minutes while the Chief finished up something on his own tablet. Finally, he took his glasses off and rubbed at his eyes. "Do you know how long I've been in cyber?"

Enzo gulped, shaking his head.

"Fifty years," Chief Brosond replied. "That's most of my life. Do you know how many times I've come across a tablet like this?"

Enzo shook his head again, and the Chief smirked.

"Once," he said, scooting Enzo's tablet across the table. "And I never got the pleasure of catching him. Since we don't know anything about you, why don't you tell me a little about who you are and why you're here."

"How do you know I won't just lie to you?" Enzo scoffed.

"I don't," the Chief said, leaning back in his chair and placing his hands together. His giant, black wings soared out on either side of him, and his small, beaked face stared at him with two dark, wide-set eyes. Brownish-black feathers lined his shoulders and down his spindly arms, his cool pale skin flashing out between tufts of down feathers. "But here's hoping."

"My name is Delphi," he responded, leaning forward to grab his tablet from the table. Sure enough, he was able to get in, but everything was encrypted. The private key was back on *Firehawk*, and only he could access it. "I've been in cyber for a hundred and fifty years, basically since its birth on Braluria."

"Impressive," the Chief said, raising an eyebrow. "I assume the key to unlock all of your information is safeguarded somewhere?"

Enzo tilted his head and gave the Chief a sardonic smile. The Chief let out a snort.

"Why are you giving me my tablet back?" Enzo asked, swiping through his various programs and finding nothing. All the data he had accumulated from his excursion was gone before he had a chance to upload it.

"Because I believe you can be of use to us," the Chief said, standing up and moving to the room's only window to Enzo's right. "Right now, we're at war with the planet's population of Ya'ados and most of their Sustri. We acquired this planet two decades ago, and ever since, they've been fighting against us."

"I wonder why," Enzo grumbled, setting his tablet down and sitting back in his chair.

"The Sustri were happy to have the burden of running this planet lifted when we came," the Chief said, turning to face Enzo with wide eyes. "Why, they practically begged for us to take it off their hands. You know how unwilling the Sustri are when it comes to responsibility."

Enzo bit his tongue and stared at the floor, a heat creeping into his face.

"Oh, don't get all pouty," the Chief scoffed and turned to sit back down in his chair. "I know not all Sustri are that way, especially you. Look at how hard you've worked to get to the level of knowledge you're at. It's very impressive."

"Why should I help you all?" Enzo asked, flicking his eyes back up to the Chief.

"Because if you don't, you'll stay in that cell for

the rest of your incredibly long life," the Chief said simply, his voice lowering into a pit of fire. Enzo sucked in a breath through his nose. He didn't doubt the Horoths had that capability.

He thought about it for a moment. Even though he didn't have any of his data unlocked, he could still gather new data and somehow get it out to Rystar and the crew if they ever moved him.

If.

"Fine," Enzo huffed, wishing he could cross his arms in defiance. "I'll help you."

The Chief grinned from ear to ear and clapped his hands together. "Excellent news. I'll have you moved to another room immediately, a nicer one on the second floor. You'll still be our prisoner, mind you, but you'll see we treat those that help us with great rewards."

Enzo felt sick to his stomach as Chief Brosond called for the guard to take Enzo away to a special cell on the second floor. He grabbed his tablet and let the guard lead him to a set of elevators that opened to a hallway lined with plush, white carpet and stained, wooden walls. The ceiling was far above them, and the guard pulled him along to a set of double doors that opened to a large, grey room with plexiglass cells plastered along its length.

Each cell was the size of a Mach II LASSO, and the cots had blankets. The toilet sat behind a half wall, and there was even a small table on the opposite wall with a chair he could lounge in.

The guard threw him in the cell and shut the door, sliding the lock shut, and Enzo was left alone to his thoughts and his tablet. He looked down at it and sighed. Even if he could break his own encryption, there was no way to get the data back to the ship. The chair squeaked under him when he sat down in it. He swiped his tablet open, diving into one of his encrypted files to try and break it open.

---

Days turned into weeks and the wind continued to howl outside.

The Horoths had him break into Sustri government files, encrypt their own files with his proprietary code, and even hide tracks as they broke into a Terran security system in Sluirossi.

Every night, he told himself it was to keep his tablet with him and crack open his files a little more.

Until week three, when it seemed the Horoths finally trusted him to do their truly dirty work. The guard came for him that morning, and he trudged out of his cell, not needing to be handcuffed now. Barely glancing up from his tablet, he stood in front of Chief Brosond and swiped away.

"Need your attention for this mission," the Chief huffed, and Enzo finished what he was doing before letting his tablet hang by his side.

"What is it today, Chief?" Enzo asked in a flat tone.

"Today, we will be performing a rehabilitation on a Ya'ados square in Sluirossi," he explained, holding a hand out for Enzo to follow him down the hall and to a different room than the one he was used to.

"What the hell is a 'rehabilitation?'" Enzo asked, his hands growing cold as he realized he was in a room with several Horoths in their classic fatigues.

"The Underground is growing a bit too rowdy for our tastes," the Chief explained. "And just like several years ago with their community center, we need to rehabilitate one of their gathering places."

"The... the Patros Community Center bombing?"

Enzo stuttered, remembering the conversation with Ji'lan and Na'gya what seemed like a lifetime ago. "They said the Sustri did that."

"So easy to dupe," the Chief chuckled and motioned for Enzo to sit down. He did, gazing up at the multitude of screens, showing the corners of streets, lone buildings, mostly centered on the Underground. His eyes lingered on the screen that showed the entrance of the Wings of Vengeance, and he shuddered. What were they up to?

"Today's target is the Ritual Family Center," the Chief said, nodding for a Horoth engineer to bring up the Center on a screen. It was bustling with people, just like most of the Underground, and Enzo turned to face the Chief, eyes wide with horror.

"You cannot expect me to assist you with this," he hissed. "These are my people."

"These are no more your people than those back on Braluria," the Chief said, his voice dripping with venom. "But you won't be performing the rehabilitation. You will be altering records that will make it seem as if the Visili Sustri were responsible."

"Who are the Visili?" Enzo asked, his eyes locked on the screen.

"An old and powerful family in Sluirossi," the Chief responded as an afterthought. He placed a hand on the console and stared at the screen that showed the Center, full of life and energy, and Enzo wanted to look away but could not. "Set the charges and countdown for five minutes."

"Yes sir," came a voice on the radio. Enzo gazed at the Horoths around him, impassive as statues.

"You can't do this," he said, standing up and clutching his tablet to his chest. "No one will believe the Sustri bombed their own people."

"They've believed it for years now," the Chief said,

standing up straight and facing Enzo. "There have always been factions of you all, and they've always hated each other. Sometimes more than they hate us. My team will send you the files you need to alter. If they're not done, expect three more rehabilitations with your signature written all over them."

It wouldn't be hard to recreate his signature, especially if they took his tablet from him. An explosion went off on the screen, and the sound of screaming filled Enzo's soul, the image of a Sustri woman walking down the street missing an arm burned into his memory forever.

He didn't stop crying that night for a long while, his face buried in his hands, back pressed against the rough fabric of his cot's blanket. The files were altered. He had sent them back to the Chief and supposed they were being sent off into the snowy void for transport. Soon enough, the Sustri would believe they had bombed themselves for no apparent reason.

He didn't think his people would be that gullible.

The Chief didn't bother him again for a few days after that and Enzo found himself with a plethora of time on his hands. He practiced his programming, tried to break his way out of the air-gapped network (to no avail), and tried fitfully to break into his files again.

He sat exhausted on his bed, weary from the solitude and from not taking a break from anything. When he closed his eyes, he saw the smoke and flames, and they shot back open to glare at his tablet again. Sitting on the edge of his bed, he turned to gaze out of the window and saw blackness, the cold penetrating the walls around him, and decided it was far too late to be awake.

Before he could lay down, a knock came at his cell door, and he whipped his head up to face the intruder. A Horoth stood there in the dimness, their wings drawn up around them.

"Na'gya?" Enzo whispered, half-standing from his bed and squinting. The face that turned to him was not Na'gya but another guard he had seen several times in the hallways.

"Who?" they asked before shaking their head. "Nevermind. I am Makeer, one of the guards on the second floor. I believe you have seen me before."

"I have," Enzo said with a nod, standing up and crossing his cell to stand in front of his door. Makeer hunched over, letting her wings create a barrier between them and the outside world as if to prevent eavesdropping. "What are you doing here."

"I have come to give you my aid," Makeer replied, her eyes darting around furtively as she spoke. "I am one of the Bedanah in hiding on Yimesotwa. We have been tasked to give our aid to enemies of the Horoth."

"Bedanah…?" Enzo repeated, digging deep in his memory for a definition.

"The Betrayers," Makeer explained, shifting her weight. "We are the ones who would not join the Terrans and assist those who are at the mercy of the Horoths now."

"But you're Horoth," Enzo said, furrowing his brow.

"We all do not have the same ideals," she said, tilting her head. "The Bedanah emerged many, many years ago when the Terrans found us. Our planet split, those that went with the Terrans in their conquest and those that stayed behind. The Ascendants, the Unaton, were the ones that joined the Terrans to the stars. We Bedanah were said to betray the Horoths in their galactic mission, dragging us back down to the depths of Chantakor."

Enzo listened, enraptured by the tale. He had heard it somewhere before, but coming from a Horoth held more weight. Nodding, he flicked his eyes up to Makeer and sighed. "How do I know I can trust you?"

"You do not," Makeer replied, shaking her head. "But I will tell you this. I know the Wings reside at 6B92 Underground, and yet they have not been... rehabilitated."

Enzo raised an eyebrow at her and shrugged a shoulder. Sure, he couldn't trust any Horoth right now, but Makeer seemed to be telling the truth, and she did know exactly where the Wings of Vengeance were holed up.

"Alright," Enzo said at last, "what is it you want me to do?"

"Keep doing what you're doing," she replied. "Keep trying to crack your code. I cannot retrieve any information from our network, but what I can do is deliver it to your friends. Do you have any data you'd like to give them now?"

"I haven't been able to hook my tablet up to the network," Enzo huffed, running a hand through his hair and glancing around, even though he knew there was no jack here. "So I have no information to give."

"Then give me a message to send to your friends," Makeer said, "and I will let them know."

"Tell them to look closer at the Ritual bombing," he said. "I know it's vague and awful, but their interest can't seem too suspicious."

"Good thinking," Makeer said with a smile. "The Chief may be a monster, but he knows brains when he sees them."

"I just know where to find stuff," Enzo said, shaking his head. "But thanks."

Makeer let their wings unfurl and stood up

straight, taking a step back from the glass. "I will let your friends know and come back when I can."

Enzo nodded and stood back, watching as Makeer left and hating the solitude again. He stood there for a few moments before heading back down to his cot and laying on it, hands behind his head.

Part of him wished he hadn't confided in Makeer, the security-oriented part. Loose lips sink ships and all that. But weeks of solitary confinement and being forced to use his skills for evil had worn Enzo down into a husk, desperate for a bit of kind contact. Even if it did come in the form of those who were keeping him prisoner.

He tried to fall asleep, his thoughts creeping to his room back on the *Firehawk* where Kyran would lay with him, though he hadn't done so in a long time. Of Rystar scooting closer to him to watch him work and the smell of space dust on her clothes. Her soft lips the last time they were alone. He sighed, folding his arms over his eyes and groaning.

It was going to be a long couple of weeks.

CHAPTER SEVEN_
RYSTAR UMARA: JERARO FARMS, YIMESOTWA

Rystar couldn't stop the guilt from creeping into her chest as she laid there with Kyran, his arm stuck under her neck and cradling her body with his other. They were naked, as per the usual, the blankets wrapped in a tangle around them.

"We should be doing something," she murmured, playing with a lock of his hair. He turned his head to gaze at her, and she let her hand fall to rest on her side.

"There's not much to do, darlin'," he muttered back, kissing her on the forehead.

"It's been weeks," she said, huffing and rolling over onto her back. Kyran pulled his arm free and sat on the edge of the bed. "What if they're doing awful things to him?"

"You heard Ji'lan," Kyran said as he stood up, "Tahi's prison isn't high security. He's probably in solitary eating crappy food."

"You don't seem too worried," Rystar said, rolling back on her side to face him and putting her head in her hand.

"I am worried," he said in a low voice, heading to

the window. "But I... well, it seems there's a lot of things I should have told you early on."

"What is it now?" she scoffed, sitting up and holding the blanket over the top half of her body.

"Enzo and I hooked when we first started flying together," he sighed, picking at a leaf of Ephrem's plant in the window. "It was once, and we decided it wasn't for us. We've been very close ever since, just not in that sense."

Rystar didn't even try to be mad and found she wasn't at all. These new-age relationships were strange, but if they got rid of her jealousy and bad feelings towards those in it, she was all for it.

"Have you two talked about it at all?" she asked, scooting towards the edge of the bed.

"We did afterward," he said, his shoulders slumping with relief. "But not since. There's not really a need to. We're friends. Always will be."

Rystar smiled, her thoughts wandering to Enzo, not for the first time. The chaste kiss he left her with, how she abandoned him at the base. Her heart filled with grief again, and she shook her head. "He kissed me, you know."

Even as she said it, guilt welled up, even though she knew what the protocol for these kinds of things was now. Kyran turned to her, eyes wide and grin plastered on his face. "Did he? I'm so proud."

"Of him?" Rystar said with a chuckle.

Kyran nodded and sat on the edge of the bed next to Rystar, and took her hand. "Of both of you. It's been so long since he branched out and made a connection with anyone else that isn't on this ship."

"And me?" she pressed. Kyran kissed her on the forehead.

"And you for breaking out of your human customs and falling for more than one person at once," he said, grinning. A flush crept into her face, and she leaned into Kyran, resting her head on his shoulder. After a while, he spoke again. "How are things coming with Na'gya?"

Rystar groaned, lifting her head up. "Not well. Every time I feel like I have a chance to tell him, he goes all weird on me and hides. I can't get him to open up. Maybe he doesn't want me to open up."

Kyran hummed, putting his arm around her and pulling her close again. "Well, if that's the case, sweetheart, he doesn't know what he's missing."

Rystar sniffed, turning her face to kiss Kyran's bare shoulder and throwing the covers off of her, heading to the bathroom. "Have to get up now. Cobalt's found another bounty for us to do today."

"When are you going to stop doing these bounties?" Kyran groaned, flopping back on the bed.

"When we have enough money to make Enzo's bail," Rystar called from the bathroom. She brushed her teeth and ran a comb through her hair before slapping on some deodorant and exiting the bathroom, picking her clothes up off a chair and pulling them on.

"Or we could take the *Krimson Princess* and bust him out, just like old times," Kyran said with a grin, standing up and letting the blanket fall to the floor.

Before Rystar could drool too badly, she sat down to pull on her socks and shoes and shook her head. "They'll shoot us down before we get to the damn prison. Besides, you said it yourself. It's probably not too bad in there for him. Just some garbage food and some solitary confinement. We'll get him out in no time."

But Rystar's mind wandered to Enzo stuck in a cell somewhere all alone because she couldn't shoot fast enough, and her heart sank.

"Don't do that, princess," Kyran said, making his way over to her as she stood up straight. He put his hands on her shoulders and rubbed her upper arms, kissing her gently before pulling away. "He'll be fine. Enzo's tougher than you think."

"I know, it's just…" Rystar started, trailing off. She shrugged and lifted up onto her toes to press another kiss to Kyran's bottom lip and crossed the room to the door. "We'll get him out. Soon."

Kyran turned to her and nodded, a warm smile still on his face. She wanted to say it, she really did, but she hadn't even fully admitted to herself just how much she loved him.

---

Cobalt waited for her near the airlock, gun in hand, as he handed it to her.

"Going to need it this time," he muttered, shoving his own in the back of his jeans and throwing on his signature fur-lined coat as Rystar pulled her own leather one on. She took the gun from Cobalt, taking in his jasper eyes and clean-cut brown hair before ensuring the safety was on and sticking it in its holster.

"Like the haircut," she commented, waiting for the airlock to open and depressurize. Cobalt grunted, and she cast a side glance at him. The sides and back had been almost completely shaved down while the top remained long and flipped over to one side. His beard was scraggly, and he scratched at it before heading out of the airlock and down the causeway, Rystar close in his wake.

She caught up to his side and matched his step. "So where are we heading today, Torlick?"

"Jeraro," he replied, taking them down the main corridor of Sluirossi towards the shuttles.

"The farms?" she asked.

"Yes," he said.

Brick. Fucking. Wall.

"Where you from, Cobalt?" she asked as they approached the shuttles and entered the queue. The next one was half an hour away, so they settled on a bench to wait. Cobalt's face flushed, and he leaned forward, elbows on his knees. "Come on, we've been flying together for a couple months now. I'd like to get to know you."

It seemed to pain Cobalt to talk, but eventually, he sat back, arms splayed out across the back of the bench, and sighed. "Braluria, like Kyran. Hometown Diaroch, few hours from Inebus."

Rystar's eyes widened, happy to get more than three words out of the guy. She stayed silent, hoping he would go on, and he did.

"Kyran found me in Inebus as a soldier," he continued. "But the war was over. I had nothing to do."

"What war?" she blurted out, eager to know more about him.

"Atrex War of Painger," he explained, "almost 200 years ago. Fighting stopped, bad feelings lingered. Left the service and began bounty hunting. That's how Kyran found me."

"Why did you go with him?" Rystar asked, and Cobalt shrugged, twisting his head to watch the shuttle pull into the station and begin to let its passengers off.

"He promised me the stars," Cobalt answered as they both left the bench and joined the queue for the shuttle. "And I've always wanted to see them."

Rystar smiled, remembering the first time she had

seen the stars in her LASSO. Normally, she refrained from using the term 'magical,' but breaking the atmosphere and seeing deep space for the first time had been the most magical experience of her life. She would go with anyone if they could give her that again.

They boarded the shuttle and sat together somewhere in the middle, staring out of the window as it pulled away from the station and into the snowstorm outside. It took nearly an hour for them to reach Jeraro Farms. During the ride, Rystar tried to find out as much about the bounty as she could.

"Sustri man," Cobalt muttered as they stood up when the shuttle stopped at the station for Jeraro Farms. "Seems he is plotting another bombing in the Underground district."

"Another?" Rystar said, remembering the bombing of the Ritual Center only several days prior.

"He is supposed to have done the Ritual bombing as well," Cobalt explained, exiting the shuttle and heading towards the main corridor. Jeraro was a smaller bubble than Sluirossi, but the farms extended many, many miles away from it, all under their own separate greenhouse. "He was last seen near Farm B52, just down there a mile."

He pointed, and Rystar groaned. The cushy, spaceship lifestyle had really done her in, and she no longer walked as much as she used to. A mile seemed like an eternity.

They passed vendors and stalls selling fresh fruits and vegetables, some Terran, some Sustri, mostly Horoth. Cobalt eyed the Horoth stalls with distaste. "See more and more of these foods now that Horoths are taking over."

Rystar hummed, watching Cobalt shudder and walk on towards a large building with a sign out front that said Tallabont Ranch. Cobalt gestured to it and made a beeline for it. "This is where he is supposed to be now."

Opening the doors for them both, Rystar followed him into the building. Inside, the ceiling stretched upwards and curved, the walls panning out on either side of them. The metal made it that much colder and stable upon stable lined the walls, their inhabitants freezing. Rystar didn't recognize very many animals and followed Cobalt down the center of the room through haystacks and giant feed towers.

"Where is he supposed to be?" Rystar asked in a hushed whisper even though no one was around.

"Around," Cobalt hissed back, taking out his pistol and hunkering down behind a pallet of grains. He flicked his head somewhere to their left. "Head that way. It looks like there's someone cleaning stalls up ahead."

With a nod, Rystar pulled her own gun out and turned the safety off, sneaking around stacks of hay and food to flank the man she now saw cleaning out a stable. She locked eyes with Cobalt across the way. He nodded, ducking out of cover and approaching the Sustri man with his gun trained.

"Darniel Visili?" Cobalt grunted, and the Sustri jumped, spying Cobalt and whipping around immediately to run. Rystar popped out of cover and trained her gun on him from his other side, and he cursed, his eyes wide and chest heaving.

"*So tamyëm,*" he pleaded, holding his hands up and speaking to Cobalt in his native tongue.

"Sure, sure, you're definitely innocent," Cobalt grunted, stowing his gun away and taking out a pair of small handcuffs, approaching the frightened man and grabbing his hands.

"They framed me," he went on in English to Rystar as Cobalt spun him around and locked his hands behind his back, slapping the cuffs on and pushing him towards the front of the building. Rystar turned the safety on her gun again and stowed it, following them out.

"Who framed you for what?" she asked, curious despite Cobalt's disinterest.

"I don't know who," he said, turning to her with pleading eyes. "But someone broke into my tablet and made it look like I was responsible for the Ritual Center bombings."

"Yeah, sure sounds like you're innocent," Rystar scoffed, rolling her eyes as they made it to the front doors and opened them. Cobalt pushed him along, but Darniel was insistent.

"I mean it," he continued.

"Then why are you in hiding?" Rystar asked him.

"Because I can't prove otherwise," he said, shrugging. "Whoever framed me used some program called Starshine, I don't even know what the hell that is. I use Python, like everyone else."

Cobalt stopped in his tracks, and so did Rystar and Darniel, who fixed him with curious stares. "What program did you say?"

"Starshine," Darniel repeated. "It's not even a real program, no one's heard of it before, but none of my family believed me. I fled here before they could turn me in."

Cobalt bowed his head, folding his arms across his chest before turning to Rystar. She raised an eyebrow at him. "What's going on?"

He lowered his voice, keeping Darniel in his sights the entire time as he bent down and whispered in her ear. "Starshine is the program Enzo created."

Pulling away, he widened his eyes at her, and she gasped, looking back at Darniel. He scoffed, shifting

CATACLYSM

his weight to another foot. "What the hell is going on?"

"I think we believe you," Rystar said, pushing him forward and motioning for them to get to the shuttles.

"You do?" he said, twisting to face her.

"Yeah, but we have to get you back to our ship as fast as we can," Rystar muttered, pressing them into the queue and hoping another shuttle would be on their way soon. She turned to Cobalt and lowered her voice. "Where did you get this bounty from?"

"The Visili family themselves," he replied, taking a step forward as the queue moved. A shuttle appeared, and the crowd began to move towards it.

"So, we can't take him back. They still think he did it," Rystar responded.

"*Telï*, we have to take him to *Firehawk*," Cobalt agreed.

They boarded the shuttle, ten times more twitchy than when they set out, and began the long ride back to Sluirossi. When they arrived, Cobalt exited first, watching for any signs of the Visili family he had received the bounty from. When he found none, he turned around and flicked his head forward for Rystar and Darniel to follow him near the outskirts of the corridor to the causeway.

They didn't run into any trouble as they approached the *Firehawk* and opened the airlock, stumbling inside and shutting the door behind them. Rystar let out a sigh of relief and tore her jacket off, watching Cobalt do the same. He faced Darniel and held up a key.

"I will release you now," Cobalt said, eyebrow raised. "It would best serve you to stay with us."

Darniel gulped and nodded, holding his hands out to Cobalt, who took his cuffs off and stowed them away in his locker. Rystar beckoned for Darniel to follow him down the hall and towards the bridge, where no one but Lupe sat. Rystar waved to them and called. "Seen Kyran anywhere?"

"*Lë yäk am yarno chu* Shea," they replied and flicked their head up to Darniel. "*Ni is rïr?*"

"Our bounty," Cobalt grumbled, pushing him towards the elevators and entering and speaking to Rystar. "They're up in the kitchen." Rystar followed and hit the button to take them there.

When the elevator doors opened, she spotted the two immediately and headed over. Kyran stood up but focused his attention on the newcomer, his brow furrowing. "Please don't tell me this is your bounty."

"It is, but listen," Rystar started, holding a hand up to quell Kyran's protests. "We think he's innocent."

"Well, that doesn't damn matter. You give him back, and they give you the money. That's how it works, sugar," Kyran scoffed, folding his arms.

"Starshine," Cobalt grunted, sitting down in a seat across from Shea and folding his arms across his broad chest. Kyran stopped and looked over to him, mouth half-open.

"What's this guy got to do with Starshine?" Kyran asked.

"I was framed for the Ritual Center bombing by someone using this program called Starshine," Darniel explained, leaning against a center column. Kyran shook his head and focused on Cobalt.

"Why would Enzo do that?" he asked, breathing heavy and turning to face Cobalt. "Why would he frame a Sustri for a bombing?"

"*Ruwe*," Cobalt said, tapping a finger to his temple. Kyran stopped, letting his hands fall to his sides.

"The Sustri have never been responsible for bombing Sluirossi," he breathed, turning to face

Darniel. "It's always been the Horoths, framing Sustris for shit they didn't do."

Cobalt nodded and turned to Darniel, whose eyes had gone wide. "You mean... even the Patros?"

"I can only assume," Kyran said, placing one hand on his hip and scratching the back of his head with the other. "*Sipe*. Why would Enzo be helping the Horoth do such things?"

"He probably has no choice," Rystar said with a shrug, crossing the room to grab a drink.

"Everyone has a choice, Umara," Kyran said, turning to face her with deadly eyes.

"Sometimes you really don't," Rystar repeated, opening the bottle of Charlom and pouring herself a drink. "He might be doing the lesser of two evils."

"Still evil," Kyran muttered, approaching her to take the bottle and pour a drink of his own.

"I wouldn't blame him," Rystar said, fixing him with a look of her own and taking a sip of her drink.

"So what are we going to do?" Darniel asked, spreading his hands. He had amber eyes like Enzo's that glowed when he spoke. A dark mop of hair that fell in his face, and Rystar regarded him as she sat down to nurse her drink.

"We tell the Wings," she said, turning to her crewmates in turn and receiving affirmative nods. She stopped on Shea. "You've been quiet this whole time. What's up?"

Shea took a moment, staring down at his tablet for a while before speaking. "I think Enzo's in trouble. I know we thought he was just having a rough time up there on Tahi, but I truly believe the Horoths have got him caught up in some terrible things. We have to save him, and soon."

"We don't have the money," Cobalt said from

across the table, and Rystar nodded, fiddling with her Cortijet before taking a drag.

"We might have to look at other options that don't involve bail and do involve a more aggressive approach," she said, tilting her head. Cobalt sighed and nodded.

"Two of us could take the *Krimson Princess* up there and try to break in," Shea suggested, and Rystar shook her head.

"Those things can barely make it into space, much less a damn moon, especially one so old," she said. Sure, the Mach II's were the humans' first attempt at a spacefaring craft, and they had done their job well, but after 60 years, they began to break down, and border gate rides became rather rough.

"We could do a stealth fly by with the *Firehawk*," Kyran said, plopping down in a chair and swirling his drink around. "Quick in and out."

"We don't even know where he's being held," Rystar said with a sigh. "I don't know how good my hacking skills are, but I can sure as shit social engineer my way into the prison and say he needs to be transferred."

"They wouldn't let him go with anyone who isn't a Horoth," Kyran said. They lapsed into silence for a moment, running out of ideas, until Lupe's voice came over the speakers and addressed them all.

"Captain, we have visitors. They're Horoth."

## CHAPTER EIGHT_
RYSTAR UMARA: SLUIROSSI, YIMESOTWA

"Horoth?" Kyran said, jumping up from his chair like it shocked him.

Rystar's heart skipped a beat as she downed her drink and stood up. No sense wasting it if the Horoths had found them. Kyran stalked to the wall and pressed a button to summon Lupe.

"Ask them what they want," Kyran whispered into the receiver, and Rystar couldn't help but snort.

"Give me a second, *antsuo*," Lupe replied and went silent for a moment. When they came back, their voice was hushed. "They said, '*te itek lïch yal lowï si sitsïch , i nye wehu näp nachíffip lïch yal tsër tsiny ru tsichíffip iyal.*"

Kyran went pale and let his hand drop from the wall as he rushed to the other side of the room and towards the airlock. Rystar bolted after him, cursing under her breath. When they reached the airlock, Kyran fumbled with the buttons until it opened. They were met with three Horoth, standing tall with their wings huddled up around them in the cold.

"Where is he?" Kyran said, catching his breath.

"He is safe, for now, but I don't know for how

long," the Horoth in the middle replied. "My name is Makeer. I have come at great risk to myself to assist you."

Kyran narrowed his eyes but stepped aside, allowing them through the airlock and into the ship. He walked them back to the elevator and to the bridge where Lupe stood at the console, hands on their hips.

"Kyran, what the hell is going on? Why are there Horoths on our ship?" they asked, throwing a hand out towards the offending party. Shea and Cobalt appeared, circling them. Kyran sighed and walked down the steps.

"They know Enzo, and Enzo trusts them," Kyran said, sighing.

"Because of what they said?" Lupe asked.

"Yes," Kyran replied, nodding. "Enzo wouldn't tell anyone that unless he was desperate."

"If you say so," Lupe said with a shrug and sat down. Rystar, on the other hand, wasn't having it.

"So what, we trust these guys now?" she blurted out, waving at the three Horoth who stood near the elevator, shuffling their feet. "After what they did?"

"We are not the Unaton," Makeer spat out, holding her head high and placing her clawed hands on her hips.

"What?" Rystar asked, shaking her head.

"The Ascendants," Kyran explained with a wave of his hand. "The Horoth that chose to go with the Terrans into space and fight everyone. These guys must be hidden Bedanah. Horoth who refuse to participate in the Horoth's conquests." He added at Rystar's questioning look.

"How the hell do you know all this stuff?" she asked.

"You'd do well to know it, too," he said, pointing a

finger at her and approaching Makeer. "It's important. Where is Enzo?"

"In the Tahi Prison," she said, towering over him. Her wings were bright red and gold, almost the same color as Kyran's eyes, and her skin was shiny and gold-dusted, with hints of orange and red. She radiated beauty, and Rystar couldn't keep her eyes off of her. "But they will not let anyone transport him."

"What about you all?" Kyran asked, flicking his head to the Horoth party.

"We are too low in status to move prisoners, especially one as important as Enzo," she said, hanging her head and shaking it, making the bangles in her ears jingle.

"Important?" Rystar repeated.

"They are using his talents to their advantage," Makeer replied with sorrow in her gold eyes.

"Shit," Rystar hissed, glancing over at Cobalt. "They must have him covering their tracks when doing the bombings. That's what Darniel was framed for."

"*Tsesuli*," Cobalt grunted, cracking his knuckles.

"Exactly," Makeer said, nodding. "Enzo is a genius. They will not want to let him go without some convincing."

Rystar pondered for a moment, putting her hand over her mouth and tapping her foot. No one on the ship was near Enzo's level of programming or cyber skill, but with all of their heads together, they might just be able to pull it off.

"What if we fabricated our own message?" she began, turning to face Kyran. "From a higher up Horoth back on Sluirossi. We say we need his talents to perform some complicated thing and have him transported to the Wing's headquarters instead."

Kyran rubbed his chin and flicked his eyes up to

Makeer, who had raised her eyebrows. "That might actually work... do you think we'd be able to create something like that, something that's believable?"

"We have Makeer," Rystar said and pointed. "All we'd need is a different ship to transport him, one with a Horoth signature."

"I'm afraid we cannot help you with that," Makeer said, "but we can help you with the Horoth message. I am in touch with several higher-ups in the Sluirossi government and can use one of their names to fabricate a message. Be aware, they will eventually catch on. We will need to be quick."

"Of course," Rystar said with a curt nod. "Kyran, Cobalt, come with me to meet with Ji'lan. We have to tell him about the Sustri being framed. We'll bring Darniel with us." They affirmed and headed to the elevator while Rystar turned to Shea. "Shea and Lupe, stay here and work with Makeer to get that message out."

"What about the ship?" Lupe asked. Rystar frowned in thought.

"Look around and see if you can find one," she replied with a shrug. "Don't you have ship contacts or something?"

"Just because I'm a pilot doesn't mean I know where every ship on sale is," Lupe chuckled and spread their hands, "but I'll definitely start looking around. There's got to be one that used to be Horoth around this place."

Rystar thanked him and took Makeer's hand in hers. "You've given us hope, and for that, I can't thank you enough."

Makeer bowed her head and smiled, her beaked nose partially hiding it. "We will do whatever is necessary to liberate this planet for our Ya'ados and Sustri *chik'i*."

Rystar gave her a warm smile and headed to the elevator that would take her to the airlock.

---

"I'm sorry, but Ji'lan is busy."

Rystar rolled her eyes. Lo'varth had become her biggest pain in the ass on Yimesotwa, even more so than the Horoth at times. She stomped a foot and craned her neck around to see Ji'lan's door stuck shut and huffed.

"This is important," Rystar insisted, placing a hand on her hip while Kyran and Cobalt stewed behind her. Darniel lingered to the side of them, and while Lo'varth didn't seem to be very afraid of Kyran, he gulped when Cobalt growled and cracked his knuckles.

"If you tell me what it's about, I'll let Ji'lan decide if it's important or not," Lo'varth said, raising his eyebrows and crossing his arms.

"It's about the Ritual Center bombing," Rystar said and pointed to Darniel, "and this is the Vasili member who was framed."

"This is a Vasili?" Lo'varth asked, his eyes widening to the size of dinner plates. Rystar rolled her eyes and groaned.

"Yes, that's what I've been trying to tell you," she huffed. "We need to get him to Ji'lan immediately."

"Fine, fine," Lo'varth said, finally caving and motioning for the party to follow him to Ji'lan's door. He knocked several times and waited until Ji'lan called for them to come in. He was sat in his chair, drink in hand, and staring at his tablet.

"I asked you specifically to let me have a day of rest, Lo'varth," he sighed, setting his tablet down and glaring at the encroaching party. When they all entered, Ji'lan's eyes fell on Darniel, and he bolted from his chair, drink spilling over the floor. "How dare you show your face here. How dare you bring him here!"

Rystar blanched but held her ground, putting herself in front of Darniel and holding up a hand. "Please, wait and listen, Ji'lan."

"You better have a damn good explanation for bringing that… that murderer to our doorstep, Umara," Ji'lan hissed, his eyes darkening with storm clouds.

"The Horoths framed him for the bombing," she explained as she quick as she could before Ji'lan exploded. "Just like they've been framing the Sustri for every bombing since the Horoth's arrival and takeover on Yimesotwa."

"And what is your evidence of this?" Ji'lan asked, his eyes losing some of their ferocity but remaining clouded over.

"Enzo," Kyran said, taking a step towards him. Ji'lan's eyes turned to Kyran, and he softened.

"How do you know it was your friend?" Ji'lan said.

"The Horoth have been forcing him to cover up their tracks with the bombings," Kyran explained, "and we were visited by some Bedanah."

"The Bedanah are here?" Ji'lan asked, raising an eyebrow.

"They said Enzo has fallen into the Horoth's hands, and they will use him to keep covering up the bombings," Kyran said, pleading with Ji'lan now. Rystar's heart broke at how much he missed having Enzo on the ship and in his life. It had been over a month now. They were all feeling the hole where Enzo used to be.

"Do you have a plan to get him back?" Ji'lan continued, turning to pick up his tablet and swiping through it.

"They won't let anyone but Horoths transport him," Rystar said, "but Makeer said she would try and fabricate a message from some higher up Horoth to send to the Tahi prison and convince them to transport Enzo down here."

"Makeer?" Ji'lan blurted, his eyes whipping up to focus on Rystar.

"Yes, she's one of the Horoths that came to us," Rystar replied, narrowing her eyes. "Do you know her?"

"I don't know a Makeer," he mumbled, focusing back on the tablet. Rystar turned to Kyran, who merely shrugged.

"Anyways," Rystar went on, "all we need now is a Horoth ship to transport him in, and we'll be all set."

"Just a Horoth ship?" Ji'lan chuckled.

"Easy, right?" Rystar said, rolling her eyes. Ji'lan hummed, placing a finger to his lips in thought.

"It might be," he said, "if you know how to hotwire LASSOs."

"I said a Horoth ship, not a LASSO," Rystar repeated.

"Yes, but lately, the Horoth have been using a new human ship, made especially for Horoths," Ji'lan explained, opening a new window on his tablet and searching for something. When he found it, he pushed the tablet to Rystar, and she gasped.

"This is the ship that killed my Mach III," she breathed. On the screen sat a Mach IV, but much smaller and more aerodynamic, its guns the main feature. She looked up to Ji'lan. "What is this called?"

"It is the Mach 4.5 Ocelot," he said.

"It's so small," she said, tilting her head. "How is it made for Horoth?"

"Ceilings are taller to accommodate wings," he said, pointing to the picture. "It's also wider. It only allows for two Horoths, but I bet three Terrans or three Sustri could easily fit."

He quirked up the corner of his mouth at the three of them and took his tablet back.

"So where do we find one of these?" Rystar asked, shaking her head.

"We were able to see one driving outside a week ago," he said, sitting back down in his chair. "My guess is it patrols the Sluirossi bubble. Two Horoths shouldn't be too hard to handle for the three of you, correct?"

Rystar gulped and turned to Kyran and Cobalt, both wearing deadly grins.

---

It didn't take too long for them to change into their snow and space suits and head out of the hidden door that led to the outside of the bubble. The snowstorm wasn't nearly as bad today as it had been, but the cold still chilled them to the bone as they began to walk the perimeter of the bubble.

"Ocelot will need a station to fuel up at," Cobalt said in her ear, and she nodded, squinting through the grayness of the storm.

"Do you think it'll be near the bubble or out a ways?" Rystar asked.

"Near bubble," Cobalt replied. "Don't want to stray too far in case they get stranded."

"Alright," Rystar said and clapped her hands together, "let's find this thing and get out of the cold."

They trudged through the blinding snow that gathered near their shins and made very slow progress. After a few hours, a dark shape appeared in the distance, and they all whooped, happy to finally get a break from the cold. As they approached, they were able to make out more details. It was a huge garage that could house the Ocelot. They tried the door, finding it open.

"That's dumb luck," Rystar muttered, and they filed inside, keeping their helmets on. Once inside, they saw an empty open space with one office near the far wall partially hidden behind a column. Cobalt crept to it and peeked inside, giving them the thumbs up when he had determined it clear.

"How long do you think we'll have to wait?" Kyran asked as they brushed the snow from their suits.

"Couple hours at least," Cobalt said with a shrug, and Kyran and Rystar groaned. "Be patient, you two."

Rystar was anything but patient.

Several hours passed, and Rystar thought she heard a soft snore coming from Kyran at one point. Finally, the garage door banged and began to open, and the three of them jumped from their seats, pulling out their guns and hiding behind a column.

The Mach 4.5 was far smaller than its Mach IV counterpart, only slightly larger than the *Krimson Princess*. It rolled in the garage on the Land setting, its massive wheels already melting the snow on them from the friction. It stopped with a squeak, and the garage door rumbled shut.

The door of the Ocelot opened, and two Horoths came clambering down, hopping with ease to the floor. They began to speak in their native language. When it was clear there were only two, Cobalt and Rystar emerged from their hiding place and trained their guns on the Horoth.

Instead of holding their hands up, which would have been the smart thing to do, they reached to their sides to grab their own guns. Both Rystar and Cobalt let off shots, hitting the Horoths square in the chest, and they fell to the floor, dark purple blood pooling underneath them.

Rystar's stomach clenched. She shook her head to get rid of the encroaching nausea. Killing wasn't something she enjoyed doing, even when necessary. She helped Cobalt with the bodies, checking them for keys and ID passes before they tossed the bodies out back and buried them in the snow.

Back inside, she turned to face the Ocelot, and her eyes went wide, able to take it all in now.

The white-gold shone at them in the dim light of the garage, its tinted black space shield impossible to see through from the outside. The wheels had deep treads and lifted it up about 7 feet from the ground, and its carefully balanced wings shot out behind it like a majestic bird.

"She's beautiful," Rystar sighed.

"She should be yours," Kyran said, putting a hand on her shoulder. Rystar turned to him, an enormous grin plastered on her face that he couldn't see, but she hoped could sense all the same.

They all climbed up the short ladder and into the Ocelot, finding more than enough room for the three of them before taking off their helmets and snow suits, leaving the space suits on underneath. Inside was a wide room, fit for a couple of Horoths, the beige interior of the walls and center console brand new and smelling like fresh leather.

"Damn, how new is this thing?" Rystar asked, running her hands over the captain's chair, not a scratch on its beige covering.

"Not sure, but we better get out of here while we can," Kyran said, hopping in the left seat. Cobalt took the right, and Rystar sat in the center, using the keys to start the engine and letting her hands hover over the console.

"Okay, this is a little different," she chuckled, sweat breaking on her forehead. The console lit up. A 3D graphical interface sprung from the screen, a holographic representation of the garage appearing. She tilted her head and watched as the garage door began to light up and held out a finger to touch it. The ship shuddered, and a voice sounded in the cabin around them.

"Garage door, open," it said in a lovely, sing-song voice.

"That's going to be annoying," Kyran said, rolling his eyes.

"I think it sounds nice," Cobalt said with a shrug.

Using the knowledge she had of the Mach III and from Lupe piloting the *Firehawk*, Rystar managed to put the Ocelot in reverse, and a camera came up, the snowstorm outside visible on its screen. She pulled the throttle, and they bumped into motion, the Ocelot grinding slowly into the snow. When it was fully out, she touched the garage door and watched it slide shut.

*Damn, this thing was impressive.*

She turned the throttle and the humongous wheels turned underneath them, twisting in the snow. Pushing down, they turned right and moved forward, clear of the garage and the holographic illumination changed to rough terrain, gliding past as they barreled forward through the storm.

"This ride is smooth as hell," Rystar commented as they approached the hidden door of the bubble, blowing past it in search of the spaceport. "Let's see if we can call Lupe."

Hands flying over the console, she finally decided to just talk to the ship on a whim.

"Uh... Ocelot?" she tried, continuing forward to the spaceport.

"*Wewtu na wo ping*," the voice around her echoed.

"Shit, it's in Pak'uian," Kyran chuckled and stopped at Rystar's look. He coughed and furrowed his brow before speaking again.

"Um... *lilm nub... p'olch* Terran," he stuttered. A moment passed before the ship's Virtual Interface spoke again.

"Language changed to Terran," it said, and they all breathed a sigh of relief.

Rystar cleared her throat and raised an eyebrow at Kyran. "We need to change your ownership to me. Can you tell me how to do that?"

"Please enter authority code," it said, a numeric pad opening at the bottom of the console.

"Oh," Rystar said, pulling out the Horoth's pass she had dug out from their pockets. She flipped it over and, with a sigh of relief, saw a scribbled number on the back of it, punching it into the numeric pad.

"Authority code accepted, please state your name and faction," the voice went on.

"Rystar Umara, Earth," she said, looking over to Kyran and raising her shoulders.

"Think it's okay to use your real name?" he asked under his breath.

"Probably shouldn't have," Rystar muttered, biting her lip. "But if it's not pinging out to the galactic network, it should be fine."

"Connecting to the Galactic Internetwork," it said, the numeric pad disappearing.

"Damn," Rystar mumbled.

"Error," the computer said after a moment. "Rystar Umara, faction: Earth, status: deceased. Please enter a different name and faction."

"Deceased?" Rystar cried.

"Hey, that's a good thing," Kyran said, placing a hand on her shoulder. "Whoever tried to kill you thinks they succeeded."

"Until now," Rystar said darkly. She tapped her foot on the floor for a moment and spoke again. "Kyran Skylock, Chantakor."

"Connecting to the Galactic Internetwork," it said again, and they rode in silence for a few seconds. "Permission granted. Welcome to the Mach 4.5 Ocelot, Kyran Skylock."

"Pleasure's all mine," Kyran said in that particular drawl of his. Rystar elbowed him in the arm.

"It's still my ship," she warned, and Kyran huffed. She laughed and widened her eyes at him. "You already have one!"

"But this one is so nice," he whined but smiled, and some of the anxiety plaguing Rystar's mind melted away.

"Ocelot, open a communications channel to DSV *Firehawk*, ship code P4-846231," Rystar asked into the console.

"Opening communications channel to DSV *Firehawk*," the ship replied as a pleasant ring wafted through the air.

"Oh, that's nice," Kyran said, head bobbing along with it.

"DSV *Firehawk*, state your name and intention," Lupe answered.

"Lupe, it's us," Rystar said. "We got the Ocelot and are on our way to you now. Open the ship hangar so we can get inside."

"That's amazing!" Lupe cried, and she heard Shea whoop in the background. "Opening up the hangar, see you soon."

The comms channel closed, and the three of them

plowed on through the snow until they reached the ship hangar and were granted clearance. Rystar held her breath the entire time, but the numbers on the Horoth's passes seemed to work. *For now.*

They found the *Firehawk* with its own hangar open, and they rolled up it, parking in the place where the *Gloriosum* used to sit. Rystar powered down the ship. They headed to the door, filing out one by one as the *Firehawk* hangar closed and Lupe and Shea came running from the door.

"Holy crap, look at that thing," Shea breathed, his eyes raking over the Ocelot.

"She's gorgeous," Lupe agreed, setting their hands on their hips and looking on in wonder.

"What are you gonna name her, Umara?" Kyran asked, throwing an arm over her shoulders. Rystar nodded her head and took the Ocelot in, hoping to keep her for a long, long time.

"*Cataclysm.*"

# CHAPTER NINE_
RYSTAR UMARA: YIMESOTWA

With the new information Ji'lan held, the Ya'ados formed a new trust with the Sustri and joined forces, their numbers overwhelming the tiny base in the Underground. Ji'lan sat in his chair, drink in hand like always, and swiped through his tablet as Rystar, Na'gya, and Kyran sat on the couch opposite him.

"So our plan is…" Rystar checked her tablet for the instructions Ji'lan had sent to her and the crew via a secure channel, taking a drag from her Cortijet, "…kick their ass and take their base."

Ji'lan let out a hearty laugh and slapped his knee. Not for the first time, Rystar wondered how many drinks he'd had. She supposed at this time of night, and considering the circumstances, she couldn't blame him.

"Sounds like a memo I'd give out," Kyran chuckled.

"Don't be *ngalm*," Ji'lan said and poured himself another drink. "I would never send out real instructions over any channel, no matter how secure it is. As your Enzo taught me, nothing is 100% safe."

A sad smile appeared on Kyran's face, and Rystar was glad that they were on their way to rescue Enzo the following day. Makeer had lent them two Horoth guards to take with them to keep up appearances on their new ship when they picked up Enzo.

The message had been fabricated and sent to the warden at the Tahi Prison. So far, they hadn't encountered anything that would indicate the Horoths were onto them. Tonight, they would celebrate, tomorrow they would kick ass.

"Are you sure you cannot spare a body for me tomorrow?" Ji'lan asked after a moment to Rystar.

"For what?" she replied. "I don't think you ever asked."

"My apologies, then," Ji'lan said, bowing his head. "The Sustri and Ya'ados are uniting forces tomorrow to take over Chure while you are rescuing Enzo."

"That's a big deal," Rystar said, her eyes widening.

"Yes, and I would be eternally grateful for any extra firepower you could lend us," Ji'lan said.

"I will stay with you and fight," Na'gya said almost immediately, sitting up straight on the couch. Ji'lan smiled and held his drink up to him.

"Spoken like a true Ya'ados," he said, "I am grateful our fates brought us together."

"Kyran, Shea, and I will be going to Tahi tomorrow," Rystar interjected, "so I'm afraid we can't help you. Cobalt might be up for it."

"I'll ask him now," Kyran said and swiped on his tablet to message Cobalt.

"Another formidable ally," Ji'lan said with a smirk.

"He says anything to get him off the ship and into battle," Kyran read off, chuckling and putting his tablet away. Ji'lan shook with laughter that ended with a sigh, fixing them all with a sad stare.

CATACLYSM

"Are you sure you and your crew cannot stay with us beyond this?" Ji'lan asked.

"We have to get Na'gya to the Hoop," Kyran said, shaking his head. "Or else we would stay here with you and fight."

"I presume the farms will be easy to take back, but we are going to need some help with the Sluirossi," Ji'lan said. He scratched at his head and set his drink down.

"Help from who?" Rystar asked, raising an eyebrow.

"It's getting late," Ji'lan burst out, and Rystar rolled her eyes. She hated mystery. "We must have a good night's sleep for tomorrow's events. Please keep in contact, we will want to know what happens with Enzo, and I am sure you will want to know the status of our takeover."

"Absolutely," Rystar said, standing up and holding out her hand to take Ji'lan's. He shook it, and Kyran's and Na'gya's in turn before crossing the room to hold the door open for them.

They exited and made it back out to the Underground, weaving through the throngs of people that never seemed to thin out, no matter how late it was. As they got back to the ship, Rystar bid goodnight to Kyran, who jetted straight for his room, and she found herself in the locker room alone with Cobalt. She steeled herself for another dead-end conversation until she jumped at Cobalt's low voice.

"He's extra sad these days," he said, setting his boot on a bench and untying it. He cast her a quick glance before focusing on his shoes again. "Without Enzo, we are all dead in the water, it seems."

"I miss him, too," Rystar admitted, taking her coat off and stowing her gun in a locker. She eyed Enzo's locker, unused for over a month now. "We'll get him tomorrow, I promise."

"Don't make promises you can't keep," he grumbled and set his shoes in his locker, stepping towards her with care.

"I tend not to," she said, closing the door to her locker and turning around to face him. An actual brick wall, he stood almost a half foot above her, reddish-orange eyes roaming over her face delicately. Rystar tilted her head and returned the gaze, sucking in a breath when his lips parted.

But nothing ever came, and she let out a sigh as Cobalt walked backward from her and towards a door near the back of the locker room. He held up a hand, signaling his departure. "*Nätsítnï arnë*, Umara."

"See you tomorrow," she called after him and leaned back against her locker, taking out her Cortijet to puff on it. Rystar had assumed Cobalt held no interest in her, but as time wore on, it seemed the opposite was true. The lingering looks, the random gifts of guns. She'd been so caught up in how Kyran and Shea and Na'gya felt about her, she had basically forgotten about the rest of the crew.

And now Enzo was gone.

She sighed and pushed away from the locker, carrying her coat out of the room and towards the elevators.

---

Makeer met them at the airlock first thing in the morning.

"And by first thing in the morning, they meant ass crack of dawn," Rystar huffed into the receiver of her tablet. Lupe sighed.

"I'm not happy about it either," they said with a yawn. "But it's time to get our asses up and moving. Enzo can't wait anymore."

"Roger that," Rystar said, sitting up and stretching.

"Who?" Lupe asked.

Rystar snorted and hung up, running a hand through her hair and taking a second to wake up, Enzo be damned.

Shoving herself into her clothes, she sped to the bathroom to freshen up before pulling on her boots and exiting her room, running into Na'gya in the hallway. "You ready?"

Na'gya's face went a paler shade than normal, and he took in a deep breath but nodded, wings fanning out behind him with pride. "I'm confident we'll take over Chure today. With the Sustri at our side, finally, I believe we'll be able to hold it."

"I know you'll do it," she said, laying a hand on his shoulder and squeezing. With a tight smile, she shook her head. "I just wish we were there to fight alongside you."

"Enzo is more important," Na'gya assured her and motioned for them to start walking down the hall. "You'll do well on that mission today."

"Thanks for the support," she said, loading onto the elevator and pressing the button for the kitchen. It opened. They saw Lupe already serving breakfast to the rest of the crew, and they joined them at the table. Two cups of coffee were pushed in front of them, and Rystar nodded her thanks, taking the coffee and sipping on it.

"Took your time today, sweetheart," Kyran said, pushing a bit of hair from his face and sipping on his own cup, empty bowl in front of him. Rystar shrugged and thanked Lupe as they set a bowl of what looked like hot cereal in front of her.

"What's this, Lupe?" she asked, taking her spoon and dipping it gently into the bowl.

"Found it in a Terran shop the other day," they responded, leaning against the counter and picking up their bowl of food again. "Supposed to be some kind of wheat cereal? I don't know, it doesn't look appetizing to me. Hope I made it right, though."

Rystar took a bite and sighed, the tastes of Earth coming back to her. She shoveled another bite in her mouth, and Kyran chuckled.

"Well, I think you did a good job, Lupe," he said, draining his drink and setting it on the table. Kyran leaned forward and clasped his hands together, addressing the crew as they fell silent. "Today's a busy day, folks. Rystar, Shea, and I will be taking the Ocelot and the two guards Makeer sent us and rescuing Shea from the Tahi Prison. Na'gya and Cobalt will be joining Ji'lan in his conquest to take over the Chure bubble. How he plans to do this, I have no idea. I'm sure it'll be fun."

"We're ready," Na'gya said, thrusting his chest out and letting his wings splay wide. Kyran smiled, a genuine thing appearing on his face, and touched two fingers to his temple in a salute.

"Let's get up to the bridge and meet with Makeer then," Kyran said, pushing himself out of his chair and hanging back a moment to address Lupe. "You make sure this thing is gassed up and ready to go. We might need to make a quick getaway."

"Will do, Captain," Lupe said, nodding and setting their bowl on the counter.

"Let's go," Kyran said, waving them all to the elevator. Rystar pushed the last few bites into her mouth, groaning at having to leave so quickly. She was able to wash it down with a final sip of coffee and make it to the elevator before the doors closed.

Up on the bridge, the three Horoths turned to face them as the elevator doors opened and the crew exited. Kyran turned to face Na'gya and Cobalt, grasping their hands one at a time. "Good luck, my friends."

"Same to you," Na'gya replied while Cobalt grunted. The two headed off to the locker room, and Rystar waved at the pair of them before they disappeared.

The Horoths approached them, and Kyran turned, placing his hands behind his back and regarding them. "And who do we have here?"

"This is Terrond and Ba'lief," Makeer introduced them. Both had solid black wings and claws, their matching high foreheads speckled with silver. Their eyes glittered green and focused on each of the crew in turn before settling back on Makeer. "They will be your guards while picking up Enzo today. Terrond is a licensed Mach 4.5 pilot and will stay on the ship while Ba'lief will be the one to interface with the guards on Tahi."

"Sounds good to me," Kyran said before putting a hand on his hip. "One flaw in our plan. We all ain't going to fit in that little Ocelot."

Rystar thought about it for a moment before cursing under her breath. "Damn it, you're right. I'll go with them. You two stay here with Lupe and monitor from afar. I'm sure everything will go smoothly."

"Like hell you're going by yourself," Kyran said, all but stomping his foot. "If anyone's going to pick up Enzo, it's me."

"It's not your ship they're flying, Kyran," Rystar said, her eyes wide and not liking the overprotective Kyran in front of her now. Kyran narrowed his eyes at her but shook his head, mouth set in a thin line before he pushed past them and down the stairs to the center console of the *Firehawk*.

A tinge of guilt picked at Rystar, but she shoved it away, turning around to face Kyran as he pouted and stared out of the space shield. Walking down the steps, she stopped behind him and lowered her voice. "I know this is important to you. That's why I want to do it, to show you I'm capable and trustworthy."

"I already know those things," Kyran sighed, still staring into the swirling snow. "It's those things *I* need to prove to *you*, not the other way around."

"You've proven yourself more than you think you have," Rystar said, pushing his shoulder so he could face her. "Let me do this for you."

"Why?" Kyran asked, narrowing his eyes at her again.

Rystar shrugged but knew exactly why.

"Keep your comms open. I'll be in touch with you," she said, leaning up to kiss his cheek before stepping up the stairs again and grabbing Shea's hand. "Keep an eye on him, okay?"

"Will do," he said with a grin, kissing her on the forehead before she flicked her head in the direction of the elevator, and she sped away, the two Horoths close behind her.

---

It was a tight fit in the Cataclysm, but they managed to squeeze in with Rystar in the center.

"I'll use my credentials to start the Ocelot up so they believe it is truly Horoth," Terrond said, punching in a code while Rystar started the ship up. The hangar in front of them opened and a torrent of snow rushed into the space around them. Rystar set the ship to space mode and lifted off from the ground, pushing forward through the hangar and out into the air.

She often wondered what the difference between Air and Space mode was, settling on the fact that maybe Space mode tightened the ship's holes more to not let in the vacuum of space. Not that she knew much about the LASSOs engineering. Maybe Kyran was right. She did need to expand her knowledge more.

As they jetted up into the atmosphere, Terrond opened the comms to a nearby border gate and began the process of using it to jump to Tahi.

When they were first discovered, border gates were only found at the edges of habitable systems, notably Terran, Sustri, and Horoth. Still, with reverse engineering, they had been able to build them near planets and their moons for quicker travel. While the Sustri and Atrex had been building border gates for many centuries, the Terrans and Horoths had only had a hundred years to build their handful.

Her thoughts were cut short by Terrond speaking into the comms to the border gate attendee. *"Tahi Dij, tsenuh nícho 548-6329-O45."*

*"Yuyl'wo chi wo tsenuh nícho, nalb letlomd p'olch wet',"* the attendee said and cut the comms.

"They said we can head to the queue now," Terrond told her.

"Not a big line for the prison, I guess," Rystar grumbled, and Terrond nodded his agreement.

"Not a very fun place to visit," he agreed.

They fell into silence as the ship in front of them blasted forward. Terrond pushed into position, waiting for the border gate's light to die down before a large, green light appeared at the top. It was hundreds of meters wide and tall and began to glow white as Terrond powered up the engines and sped through, the jump only lasting a few seconds as they appeared on the other side.

The ship in front of them wasn't too far, and they followed it to the moon where a complex sprawled across many miles of rocks and craters. They swirled down and landed in a spot designated for an Ocelot. As they set down, the platform began to shake and sink, bringing them underground and sealing them in from the vacuum above.

"Ocelot 548-6329-O45, *yur Tahi Dij, nalb lehmei wo chiybeye ping ild,*" a comms voice came in over the receiver, and Rystar's heart jumped into her throat. The Horoths on either side of her remained calm, and she tried to straighten her back, getting rid of the silliness creeping up in her face.

"Tahi Prison, this is Ba'lief Roanil, approaching our 2340 appointment to transport the prisoner Enzo Vida to the Sluirossi Headquarters," Ba'lief said without a hitch, switching to Terran so Rystar could understand them. A moment passed when Rystar could have sworn she noticed a bead of sweat on Ba'lief's forehead before the comms came back.

"Welcome, Ba'lief Roanil, someone will be out to your ship shortly," the comms said, rather pleasantly, in Rystar's opinion. She hummed and glanced to the Horoths on either side of her, who each gave her a slight smile. Rystar beamed, considering the day a victory already.

Presently, a knock sounded at the airlock, and Rystar hopped up from her seat, heading to the back of the ship where the open lockers were and hid. Ba'lief also rose and headed to the door, waiting until Rystar had fully hidden herself before opening the door. "Thank you, yes we will keep him safe. He will be returned as soon as the mission is fulfilled."

The airlock shut, and the sound of handcuffs clanging reached her ears. Rystar bounced on her toes, waiting for Enzo to come into view.

"Oh, you trust me enough to take my cuffs off *now*," Enzo huffed as he meandered into view.

"I believe you have a visitor, Mx. Umara," Ba'lief said, and Enzo whipped around to find her standing in the locker room, grinning from ear to ear.

"Rystar," he hissed, eyes going wide and launching himself forward to throw his arms around her. "What the hell are you doing here?"

Rystar hugged him back, squeezing so tightly she thought she might break a rib. They separated, and she batted a tear away before tearing towards the console. "We have to go now, come on."

"There's nowhere to sit," Enzo said, looking around. "What is this thing?"

"Ocelot, Mach 4.5," Rystar replied, turning around and tapping her nose at him. "Nice, ain't it?"

"We must hurry and depart," Terrond said, a tinge of worry in his voice.

"Right, go now, talk later," Rystar said. Terrond requested lift off from the comms while Enzo buried himself in his tablet, presumably to find out everything he could about the ship he was on. The platform they sat on twisted and lifted them up into the air, and they pushed off from it, flying away from the prison and towards the border gate. "I can't believe we did it."

"Don't count your blessings until they've been bestowed upon you," Terrond warned and pointed to the border gate queue and turning on the comms.

"Tahi border gate, this is Ocelot 548-6329-O45 requesting permission to advance in the queue for Yimesotwa," he said into the comms. The receiver buzzed for a moment and then lapsed into silence.

They all exchanged glances before Terrond hit the receiver again. "Come in, Tahi border gate, this is Ocelot 548-6329-O45 requesting permission to advance in the queue for Yimesotwa."

"Ocelot 548-6329-O45 this is Tahi border gate, permission denied, the border gate is currently closed for maintenance, you will need to take the space expressway," the voice came back, a little harried, if Rystar was honest.

"What the hell?" she said, peering at the border gate glowing white and powering down again. "Doesn't look closed to me."

"It's only a couple hours," Terrond shrugged, letting go of the throttle and allowing Rystar to take over and send them towards the expressway. Rystar groaned.

A few minutes into the ride, Enzo tapped Rystar on the shoulder and shoved his tablet in her face. "Look."

"I don't understand any of this—" she began, but he cut her off.

"Our transmission was intercepted," he blurted out, "does this thing have guns?"

"Sure, why?" Rystar asked, shaking her head at his insistence. "What the hell is going on?"

"That wasn't the border gate," he said, pressing a button on the center console to bring up a radar. Sure enough, a large vessel approached them from behind, its light blinking in wait.

## CHAPTER TEN_
COBALT TORLICK: CHURE BUBBLE, YIMESOTWA

Having spoken three words to Na'gya since his arrival on the *Firehawk*, Cobalt was having trouble formulating any now. They walked side by side with Kyran trailing the rear to the shuttles that would lead them to Chure. Most of the forces had already arrived in Chure over the past several days. Cobalt, Na'gya, and Kyran were supposed to meet Ji'lan at the station for further orders.

"Na'gya! Cobalt! Kyran!"

A high voice made them turn, and they saw Makeer rushing towards them, arm raised. They stopped and waited for her to catch up with them.

"What's going on?" Na'gya asked, eyeing her.

"I wanted to join you since I could not go with Terrond and Ba'lief," she said, catching her breath and motioning for them to continue walking. "Please, let's hurry. I don't want us to be seen together too much. I just came from the Underground."

"Why did you go there?" Na'gya asked.

"That doesn't matter now. It is burning," she said, keeping her eyes forward. Cobalt sucked in a breath of air as he side-eyed Makeer's presence.

"Burning?" Na'gya spat, stumbling in his tracks and fixing Makeer with a heated glare. "What the hell happened? Who did it?"

Makeer shook her head and quickened her pace, making the men do the same. "It must have been someone from the Underground, or someone from the Bedanah is not a Bedanah at all. They are working for the Horoth government. They must have told them where the Underground is. It is very lucky you all chose today to vacate."

"Or the leak knew we were vacating today," Na'gya said darkly. Makeer raised an eyebrow and nodded.

"Ji'lan's there," Cobalt said, pointing to a queue line and watching the bright, white wings swish around to face them.

They hurried up to him, and his eyes went wide as they fell on Makeer. Cobalt, Na'gya, and Kyran didn't exist as he approached her, hands balled into fists. "What are you doing here?"

"I thought you said you didn't know a Makeer," Na'gya said, moving to the side. Makeer tilted her head, her beautiful golden wings folding to embrace her and Ji'lan, who stepped back instinctively.

"Ji'lan, *ti'kulb*," she breathed, holding her arms out, tears filling her eyes.

"Your son?" Na'gya burst out.

"What are you doing here?" Ji'lan repeated, voice shaking.

"I have come to tell you there is a traitor in your midst," she said, letting her arms fall to her sides and raising her chin.

"Who, you?" Ji'lan said with a sneer. She didn't flinch, but a shadow flickered across her face. "The one who left my father to parade around with the Horoth government?"

"I have been, and will always be, Bedanah, *kulb*," she said, thrusting her chest out and taking in a deep breath. "It was my greatest regret to leave you both and go undercover, but necessary to the cause."

"So you cared more about the cause than your husband and child," Ji'lan countered, folding his arms across his chest.

"I'm so sorry, you two, but can we get to the point here?" Na'gya cut in, and Cobalt nodded, scratching the back of his head and twisting his head around to see if they were being followed. They were out in the open here.

"Yes, my apologies," Makeer said, bowing her head. "Your Underground base has been exposed, by who, I do not know. But you cannot go back there."

"What do you mean, exposed?" Ji'lan burst out, letting his arms fall to his sides.

"I mean, it burns as we speak," Makeer clarified.

"Who?" Ji'lan brayed. "Who did this? And why should I believe you?"

"Because I assisted in saving your friends from Tahi," she said a little more firmly. "Because for the past thirty-four years, I have been plagued with watching the Horoths bomb innocent people and take over their planets. Because it was a stroke of luck that I found you, and I do not want to hide anymore."

Ji'lan stayed silent for a moment, exchanging glances with both Na'gya and Cobalt, who nodded to him in turn before taking a deep breath and sighing. "I cannot forgive you for leaving. But you may have a chance to prove yourself today."

"I look forward to it, *ti'kulb*," Makeer said and bowed deeply, tears filling her eyes again. Cobalt looked away towards the shuttle coming in, unable to fathom what it would be like to reunite with a parent.

They all headed towards the shuttle and entered, joined by more Ya'ados and Sustri soldiers.

"How were you able to organize this?" Na'gya asked as the shuttle pulled away from the bubble and into the storm outside.

"Sustri run most of the shuttle routes here," Ji'lan explained, holding onto an overhead line and staring out of the window. Makeer stayed close behind, sharing his stare. "With their newfound alliance, we were able to have them turn a blind eye to this shuttle for the past few days while we organized at Chure."

"Do we have a base at Chure?" Na'gya asked.

"A very small one," Ji'lan responded. "Small bands of fighters have been positioning themselves around Chure and upon my arrival will strike. This is the moment we have been waiting for, for two years."

"We need to be careful how thin we spread ourselves today," Cobalt said, scratching his nose and looking up at Ji'lan. Ji'lan let out a short chuckle and patted Cobalt on the shoulder.

"You do not say much, *ti'chalch*, but when you do, it's to the point," he laughed and let his arm hang down again. "Yes, Chure is large, and our numbers are by no means at the amount I would like them to be at. But we are strong and smart. We will take over Chure this day."

Cobalt let out a huff and nodded, staring at the ground and willing the ride to be over so he could get off and fight.

Not that fighting was his favorite thing, though he excelled at it. Cobalt had always been good at fighting since his youth when he had joined the Sustri Forces at 90. War after war, he found himself jumping through them with ease, filling up the medal case in his cramped apartment in Inebus.

Until Kyran found him, broken and drunk, at a bar somewhere on Braluria's moon, Clandia.

"What have they done for you in the past 600 years, anyway?" Kyran said, downing a drink and casting a glance around the dingy space. A place like this wasn't usually packed in the afternoon hours, and at the moment, only housed a few lonely Sustri, sinking to the bottom of their bottles. Cobalt was one of them.

"Why do you care?" Cobalt grunted, holding his empty glass up to the bartender. He shrugged his shoulders and adjusted his fur-lined coat, settling down in his chair a little further.

Kyran tilted his head and swiveled in his chair, and Cobalt hadn't ever met another Sustri like him. He was different and foreign, almost as if he wasn't a Sustri at all, but Cobalt could tell from the fangs and the way his eyes glowed like embers in the dark. "Because I hate seeing what the system does to us. We put so much of our lives in their hands and get next to nothing in return."

"How long did you serve?" Cobalt asked, turning his head to face Kyran for the first time since their meeting.

"With the Sustri Forces?" Kyran said, raising an eyebrow. "None. With the Terran military, far too long."

This caught Cobalt's attention, and he sat back in his chair, nodding his thanks to the bartender. "That makes no sense."

"Not very much about my life makes sense," Kyran scoffed, pushing his empty drink to the edge of the bar. "But I'm determined to make something of myself now. And I'd like a loyal crew to do it with."

There wasn't much Cobalt wanted to do these days, much less jettison himself off into space with some weirdo Sustri he just met. But he took a drink and sized Kyran up, *frowning when he couldn't do so.* "What kind of ship you got?"

"One I acquired from Aurum," Kyran said, smiling so wide his fangs came out below his bottom lip. Cobalt let out a bark of a laugh and took his drink in one go, slapping his hand on the bar top.

"This I have to see."

Cobalt smiled at the memory as the shuttle shot into the Chure bubble and began to slow as it reached its stop. Already, he could see the smoke wafting up from distant factories and the barricades created in the streets running alongside them. The shuttle slowed to a halt. Cobalt and Kyran caught their balance before exiting, Makeer and Ji'lan close behind them.

"Where to, boss?" Kyran asked, standing on his toes to glance around at the commotion. Ji'lan pointed to a small building off to their right.

"There's where we are outfitting our soldiers," he said. "Let us head there, and I will make sure they give you the best."

"What should I do?" Makeer asked, and Ji'lan hung back.

"Stay around here for now," Ji'lan replied and placed his hand in his mother's. "I do not think my people will trust you immediately, but I will introduce you formally soon."

Makeer nodded and hung back, wings wrapped around her in a protective stance. Ji'lan motioned for them to follow him, and they made their way to the building. Once inside, soldiers and fighters alike made a space for Ji'lan to pass through and Cobalt and Kyran exchanged glances before following him deeper into the chaos.

"What is your flavor, men?" Ji'lan asked the two as

he stopped in front of a large kiosk in the middle of a foyer.

"The best you got, I suppose," Kyran said, clapping his hands together and rubbing them, eyeing the stores.

"Give them Sustri armor, the P-80 rifles, and two helmets," Ji'lan asked of the Ya'ados behind the counter. He disappeared for a moment before coming back with their respective gear, and Kyran and Cobalt nodded in approval. They moved away to the side of the foyer and began to dress as Ji'lan addressed them again.

"You will follow me down the center of the bubble to Chure's main hall," he explained as Cobalt pulled his armor on. It was light and airy and let his joints breathe, but hard enough to stop bullets and bayonets, provided the Horoth still used them. "We believe the Horoth are holding off sending reinforcements because there are not many of us, but with this new crew arriving, they might change their mind."

"So get there quick, got it," Kyran said, pulling on his helmet and picking up his rifle. Cobalt had never seen him in a full soldier getup before and wondered if this is what Kyran looked like before becoming a pirate.

"You will be joined by a seasoned Sustri/Ya'ados platoon that you will be in charge of, Cobalt," Ji'lan said, pointing at him. Cobalt nodded and snapped his helmet on, picking up his rifle and doing a quick assessment of it. Not so different from the rifles and guns he was used to.

"Why not me?" Kyran huffed, following Ji'lan out of the front doors and around the building where a platoon of around twenty fighters milled about. When Ji'lan approached them, they snapped to attention while Cobalt and Kyran hung back. Factories towered over them, and in the distance, fires burned. Cobalt craned his neck to find the center street that would take them to the capital and could not.

"*Ti'ngundo'i*," Ji'lan addressed them with his wings outstretched. Many of the fighters in front of him had wings that pressed against the backdrop of the outer bubble, its never-ending swirling snow and velvet black sky. "today is the day we take back Chure. For too long, these factories have held our people as slaves, underprivileged workers, led by the Horoth and their greed for Uranium. Today is the day we fight back and take their Capitol, take back *our* Capitol, and begin to heal."

The platoon whooped, throwing their fists in the air, a terrifying battle cry that made the hair on Cobalt's neck stand up. He hated war, but sometimes, he really loved fighting.

"Meet Cobalt Torlick, your captain for the day," Ji'lan swept a hand to present Cobalt and Kyran, who nodded at their fighters. "And his second-in-command, Kyran Skylock. You will follow their orders as they lead you to the Capitol. We will not fail this day."

The fighters whooped again, and footsteps hurried up behind them. Cobalt and Kyran turned to face the new arrivals. Ji'lan's eyes widened, and he scoffed.

"Absolutely not. Why are you not back near the shuttles?" he asked with a fire in his voice. Minabel huffed and held her helmet under one arm while the other sat on her hip.

"You cannot stop us from fighting," she said, gesturing to the platoon behind him. "This is the best you have, led by the best captain. I will join, and you will not stop me. Or Lo'varth."

Lo'varth grumbled and snapped his helmet on,

shuffling his feet in the dirt. It did not seem as if this was his choice alone, but he followed Minabel to the front of the line and stood with her, wings outstretched.

"*Ti'ngulbonj*, I couldn't stand to lose you," Ji'lan said in a hushed voice, approaching her and running a hand across her cheek. She raised an eyebrow and smirked.

"You will not, then," she said and pulled her helmet on. In spite of himself, it seemed, Ji'lan beamed and pulled his fiancee into an embrace.

Cobalt nodded, twisting to face the platoon and putting on his best war voice, one he hadn't used in many years. "We follow Ji'lan to victory. Move out."

Ji'lan pulled a helmet from the ground, his armor already in place, and snapped it on, picking up his own rifle and setting off towards the street. To their left was the main road that led to the Capitol, about two miles down and full of hostile forces.

As they approached the main road, flanked with old, rusted buildings and shops, Cobalt turned to walk backward and addressed the platoon. "Lo'varth and this side of the platoon will follow me down the left side of the road, Minabel, Kyran, Ji'lan, and the rest of you will head down the right. We advance slowly. We don't play the hero. Do we want it done fast, or do we want it done right?"

"Right!" the crew barked, and Cobalt tapped his helmet.

"Let's move."

The group split up, and while Cobalt hated doing it, at least the road wasn't too wide and they could easily see the other half of the platoon. Creeping up the sides of the street, they didn't encounter any issues for the first half a mile. Horoth troops began to appear then, jumping out from behind cars, and Cobalt shouted for them to get to cover.

He popped out, shooting his rifle and catching a Horoth in the neck, blood spraying out before he fell to the ground. The Horoth's armor didn't seem to extend to their necks, and he turned to his platoon. "Advance behind cover. Wait for me to move to the next one."

On and on they went, a slow, painful crawl down the street as Cobalt continued to advance up, punching through the Horoth troops with ease. That was Cobalt's main advantage: over 400 years of active combat, the Horoths just didn't have. The kids behind him, and he did mean kids, may have been just as green as the Horoths they were fighting.

Occasionally, he'd glance over to the opposite side of the street where Kyran and his squad moved up. Kyran was normally such a goofball, a stringy mess of drawling and nonchalance. He forgot Kyran had more fighting experience than Cobalt had. He would pop out of cover and pick of several Horoth before dropping back down and waiting for the coast to clear before advancing, and Cobalt sighed in relief at his choice to let Kyran lead.

They saw the Capitol come into view at long last, and Cobalt held up a hand, indicating for them to stop. There were about ten fighters behind them, each one in cover. As he soon learned, one of them was not in the best cover they could be. A shot rang out around them, and one of his fighters spun around, a brand new hole in their head making them drop to the ground.

"Sniper, take cover!" Cobalt called out, and his crew dropped to the ground or buried themselves further behind whatever wall they had chosen. He slid down the car he had taken shelter behind and addressed his group.

"Any snipers?" he asked. One member raised their hand from behind a concrete barrier before pulling it back quickly, the bulky gun on their back giving them away. "What's your name?"

"Ma'lik, sir," she said.

"Ma'lik, I'd like you to head into that building to our right here and go to the top," Cobalt asked. "From there, we'll try and show you where the sniper is."

"Copy that," Ma'lik said and jetted out from her cover and into the building. A shot pinged off a light post but missed, and Cobalt breathed a sigh of relief.

They waited for several minutes until the radio in Cobalt's helmet chirped on, and Ma'lik addressed the platoon. "I'm here, but no sign of the sniper."

Cobalt grunted and hit the ground next to him. He wasn't using any of his fighters as bait, that was for sure. Kyran piped up in his ear. "What's the plan, Captain?"

"I'm going to move from my cover. Hopefully, the sniper will take a shot at me," he said and steeled himself for a blow. He didn't know how hard these helmets were, but apparently not too hard, based on what happened to the last fighter who got shot.

"Cobalt, you can't," Kyran pleaded, and Cobalt watched as he danced on his toes from across the street. The radio clicked in his ear, and Kyran spoke to him directly. "I lost Enzo. I can't lose you, too."

"Enzo's not lost," Cobalt said. "Have faith. They'll bring him back. This is important."

"I know it is," Kyran said and shook his head.

From behind him, a fighter scrambled out and joined Cobalt next to him at the car, and Cobalt saw it was Lo'varth. "What are you doing?"

"I'll show you where the sniper is," he said and took a deep breath.

"Wait, stop—" Cobalt said, trying to drag Lo'varth back down, but he was too late. The bullet ripped through Lo'varth's chest, and he dropped to the ground like a stone. From up on the building, another shot rang out, followed by a loud whoop.

"I got him, sir!" Ma'lik cried, but Cobalt was busy tearing the helmet from Lo'varth's face and pulling him into his lap.

"What's going on over there?" Ji'lan cried, rushing over and skidding to sit next to Cobalt and the dying Lo'varth. "What did you do, Lo'varth?"

"*Ti ndom*," he said, a spittle of blood running down his lips. "Ji'lan, *mbu dinyu*."

"For what, my friend?" Ji'lan asked, his wings shuddering.

Before he could say what he was sorry for, the light in Lo'varth's eyes disappeared, leaving a crying Ji'lan in their wake.

## CHAPTER ELEVEN_
RYSTAR UMARA: OUTSIDE TAHI, NANYIFMIL SYSTEM

Rystar's eyes locked onto the blinking light as it approached them, and the comms receiver buzzed again.

"Ocelot Buzzkill, come in, Ocelot Buzzkill," the comms came in again, and Rystar blanched at the harsh voice. They all exchanged glances as Rystar hit the comms button.

"Identify yourself immediately," she snapped, urging the ship forward.

"Looks like someone got a fancy new ship," they said, their voice like steel wool ripping through the receiver. "Too bad you don't know how to use it. I'll tear through this one the same as I did with that piece of garbage you used to fly."

Rystar's chest tightened and her stomach dropped, a bead of sweat breaking out on her forehead, making her face clammy. "Who the hell are you?"

"Bet you didn't think the FDDS was this smart enough to catch up with you?" the voice said. "Don't worry, you don't know me. But I know all about you and Shea and that damn hybrid. And that shifty Sustri crew that took you all in."

Whatever ship their pursuer was in, and Rystar assumed it was another Ocelot, it could catch up to them as soon as she accelerated. There was no getting out of this unless they fought, and Rystar had no idea what she was doing in this thing.

"My name is Captain Marsters," he went on, and Rystar gasped. Enzo furrowed his brow at her, and she lowered her voice.

"Marsters captured Na'gya and his people before we rescued him," she said with a dawning realization. "He probably killed Ju'sif back on Yarev."

"How did he find us?" Enzo asked as Rystar glanced over the weapons systems.

"I, uh," she started, clearing her throat. "I put in my real name when transferring ownership over to me in this ship."

Enzo's eyes widened in horror. "Have I taught you nothing?"

She shrugged and winced at him. "Well, at least we have the chance now to kill the crap out of this guy and be done with it."

"Always looking on the bright side," Enzo chuckled and held on to the back of her seat. He lowered his voice and bent to speak in her ear. "Keep him talking."

She turned around to see him buried in his tablet again. "What are you doing?"

"Getting the calvary," he whispered back with a smirk. She nodded and hit the comms button again.

"Oh, sorry, was I supposed to know you?" she asked, swerving to avoid a large Mach V while passing it. The blip on her radar behind her veered as well, keeping its pace.

"You'd do well to, Umara," Marsters sneered

through the line. "I'm the one who captured that hybrid trash, and you're the idiot who let him go."

"Why do you want Na'gya so bad?" she asked, her eyes darting around for any sign of Lupe.

"Locking up hybrids isn't enough for you?" he asked with a sigh. "Na'gya's dangerous. He has the power to create a hell of revolution, one we can't have."

"What's your issue with the Ya'ados anyway?" Rystar asked, genuinely curious this time.

"They don't belong here," he said, a true venom lacing his voice. "Humans and Horoths were never meant to mix, and they've created horrifying creatures that have no business existing."

"This man is disgusting," Terrond spat, clawed hands flying over the weapons system. "I know the basics of combat, turn us around and we will annihilate him."

"Not yet. We're no match against him," Rystar said, shaking her head. She hit the comms button again. "So, you're a purist. Kind of like those folks back on Earth a couple centuries ago."

"And were they wrong?" Marsters asked.

"Yes, absolutely, that's why they lost the war and were ultimately vilified by the rest of the population," Rystar huffed, rolling her eyes at the fact these people still existed. "Who sent you?"

"An old friend of yours," Marsters said. "And he sure is pissed off at you."

Rystar furrowed her eyebrows before they shot up into her hairline and a knife shot through her heart.

*It couldn't be...*

"Rystar, everything okay?" Enzo asked, placing a hand on her shoulder. Her hands had gone clammy, and the color had drained from her as the terrifying realization smacked her across the face.

"He couldn't have ordered you to kill me," she breathed, holding the comms button down. "He wouldn't do that."

"Jorge has done a lot more than you think," Marsters spat. "Don't think for a second he was ever on your side."

Rystar had run several bounties with Jorge before his forced retirement in 2114. She had little knowledge of what he did before he ran bounties and the extent of his job and reach in the FDDS, but from his kill orders, it was clear he was much higher up than she initially thought.

"Did he order Ju'sif killed?" Rystar asked, taking a deep breath.

"Yes, and I enjoyed putting a bullet through his brain, too," came the reply, and if it were possible, Rystar's hands went even colder.

"He's here," Enzo said, squeezing her shoulder again. "End this conversation. You don't need to hear it."

"It's been fun catching up, Marsters, but I'm going to have to hand you off to my friends here," Rystar said, wiping at her nose and smiling at the large blip coming up behind Marsters' Ocelot.

"What are you talking about?" Marsters hissed before cursing as Rystar assumed he noticed the enormous *Firehawk* behind him.

"They're not as talkative as I am," Rystar assured him, slowing down some to allow the *Firehawk* to catch up to them.

"That's fine, Umara," Marsters said in a deadly voice, hissing like a snake through the airwaves to her. She shuddered in spite of herself. "I'll find you wherever you go."

Rystar's hand shook for a moment before she snapped out of it and the blip on her radar disappeared, replaced with the comforting shape of the *Firehawk* coming up next to them and then accelerating to present its hangar to them.

It opened, and Rystar pushed forward, landing with care in its designated spot and powering down. She let out a sigh that deflated her chest and let her head fall back in the chair as Enzo slid his hands on her shoulders and rubbed.

"I'm sorry you had to go through that," he said slowly as the two Horoths rose from their chairs and made to exit.

"It's fine. We just have to plan accordingly now," Rystar said, her head much clearer than she expected it to be. "I need to talk with Shea."

She placed a hand on Enzo's and squeezed for a moment before getting up from her chair and following him to the door. Descending the ladder, she jumped the last few steps to the floor and looked up to see Shea rushing towards her. "Rystar, what the hell happened?"

"We got Enzo, but some dickhead caught up to us," she explained.

"Who?" Shea asked and beckoned for them to follow her up to the bridge. They entered the elevator, and it shuddered as it sent them up.

"Guy named Marsters," she said, "but it's not him that scares me. It's who sent him."

"Who sent him?" Shea asked, his voice shaky as they exited onto the bridge and approached the center console.

"Jorge," Rystar said, her voice a stone at the bottom of the ocean. She strapped herself in as the two Horoths, Enzo, and Shea did the same. Shea went pale.

"He wouldn't order you killed," he breathed.

"He did," she said, nodding her head. "He ordered Ju'sif killed and the *Gloriosum* destroyed."

"I can't believe it," Shea whispered, turning to face the front of the *Firehawk* as Lupe turned them around to head back to the border gate.

"I kind of can," Rystar said with a shrug, the initial shock wearing off and replacing itself with anger. "We don't have any idea who that man was before he ran the bounty hunter department."

"I guess you're right," Shea said, still reeling from the news.

"Chure ground team to *Firehawk*, come in *Firehawk*," the comms blasted out, and Lupe slapped the receiver.

"What's going on, ground team?" Lupe answered.

"We need immediate assistance on the ground," the voice came through again. Rystar recognized it as Kyran's.

"Damn it, give me a second," Lupe said and switched the channel. "*Firehawk* to Tahi border gate, need transport to Chure bubble in Yimesotwa."

"*Firehawk*, this is Tahi border gate. Please join the queue. You are third in line for departure," the comms came back, and Lupe hissed, switching the channels back.

"Now, what the hell is wrong with you all?" Lupe snapped, and Kyran came back.

"Where are you?" he blurted. "You're supposed to be on Yimesotwa. You can get here in two minutes."

"Well, something went wrong with Enzo's rescue, and I had to come help," Lupe said, tapping on the console as the queue shortened as slow as it could.

"Is everything okay?" Kyran asked, lowering his voice.

"I'm fine, Kyran, good to hear you," Enzo piped up from his seat.

"Oh, thank God," Kyran sighed.

"Anyways," Lupe cut in, "I can be at Yimesotwa in 15 minutes, but I don't know how I can help you."

"Get Rystar and her sweet *Cataclysm* to burst in and tear this place to shreds," Kyran said, and the sound of guns battered on in the background. Rystar gulped, hating where Kyran was and tapping her foot restlessly.

"Can she even get that thing in the bubble?" Lupe asked, turning the engines up and waiting for the gate to turn white.

"There's a door on the side of the bubble, near the west end. I can see it from over here," Kyran said and cut out for a moment while they entered the gate and spun around, spitting out on the other side. Lupe turned and headed to the Chure bubble's west side, descending to the planet with ease.

"Suit up, I guess," Lupe said with a shrug. Rystar nodded, unbuckling herself and heading back to the elevator with Shea to take her down to the hangar. They hurried into the *Cataclysm* and turned it on, setting it to Land mode. The wheels on either side groaned and sat into place while the ship's wings swept back and the engines burst on. Once they had landed, Lupe opened the hangar door, and they headed out back into the snow.

"Alright," Rystar said, pulling into a stopping position near the bubble. "Let's see if we can find this door."

They edged along the side of the bubble until Rystar noticed the smoke and flames coming from inside the bubble, and she quickened her pace. The bubble was a large, clear dome, much like Sluirossi, except at the edge of the bubble where it met the ground. There, it was a ton of metal, sinking into the ground below it to keep the atmosphere inside. A door appeared on the edge of this metal bit, and Rystar watched as it popped up on her radar.

"I can open that," Enzo said, and both Rystar and Shea jumped, not realizing he had made it on the ship, too.

"When the hell did you get here?" Rystar asked. Enzo shrugged, sitting down in the seat next to Rystar.

"Hung out in the locker room until I was sure you wouldn't kick me off," he said. Rystar narrowed her eyes at him and turned back to face the door. "Give me a second, and I'll have it open."

True to his word, Enzo had it open in a few seconds, and Rystar drove inside, letting it close behind her and plunging them into darkness.

"By the way, do you know what's going on with the Underground?" Enzo said, suddenly concerned.

"No, I haven't had a chance to go there all day," Rystar said, shaking her head as the door in front of them opened to a world of fire and war.

"No one is answering and their network is down," Enzo said under his breath, swiping through his tablet.

"I'm sure they're busy doing…" Rystar said, waving to the scene in front of them, "…this."

Enzo looked up and gulped, nodding his understanding and going back to his tablet. Rystar continued down the road. "Ocelot, can you tell me where the Capitol of Chure is and how to get there?"

"One moment, please," the VI said, and Enzo looked up, narrowing his eyes.

"I told you he wouldn't like it," Shea chuckled and Rystar let out a small smile.

# CATACLYSM

"It's not that I don't like it," Enzo huffed. "It's just I can probably do it a lot better."

"But now I don't have to ask you for directions. You can focus on more important things," Rystar said. Enzo grumbled.

The console lit up with a route Rystar began to follow and be thoroughly impressed with. Down twisted, broken roads they went until suddenly they turned down a main road and saw the Capitol, completely surrounded by Horoth tanks and troops.

"Enzo, can you open up a comms to the ground team," Rystar said, her throat dry.

"Sure thing," he replied, tearing his eyes away from the street and opening a comms channel from his tablet to the console.

"*Cataclysm* to ground team, come in," Rystar called in on the comms, waiting with bated breath.

"Ground team to *Cataclysm*, this is Kyran. Are you close?" Kyran said over the receiver, and Rystar let out the breath she was holding.

"We have eyes on the Capitol, Skylock," Rystar responded and began the sequence to turn the weapons systems on.

"God damn, finally, where the hell have you been?" Kyran spat, and Rystar's eyes widened.

"Might want to rethink your strategy, there, Ky," Rystar shot back.

"Sorry, Umara," Kyran said, "we've been taking major hits here in the Capitol. It's nice to have some backup."

"Well, I'll do what I can," Rystar said and shrugged as the weapons system came online and the VI began to speak to them.

"Please select an assist mode," it said as the weapons flashed on the comms console in front of them.

"Um, please assist me as much as you can," Rystar said, watching the throttle disappear, and the weapons begin to flash.

"Please state an intention," the VI said. Rystar looked to Shea, who merely shrugged at her.

"We need to get to the Capitol," Rystar said.

"Affirmative," the VI confirmed, and the *Cataclysm* shot forward, guns blazing and tearing through tank after tank that dared to stand in their way. Horoths darted into the sidewalks near the street as the Cataclysm barreled through, its tires mowing down their assault vehicles and Horoths alike.

"Oh Christ, I didn't expect this," Rystar said, holding onto the console and bouncing around as the LASSO plowed forward with its guns and gigantic tires running over everything in its path.

As quickly as the assault had begun, it was over, and they skidded to a halt outside of the Capitol's steps at an angle, partially facing the street they had just annihilated. Both Shea and Enzo were still holding on for dear life, and Rystar unbuckled herself, rising from her seat and patting the console.

"Thanks, Ocelot," she said and headed to the locker room for her jacket and pistol.

"You're welcome, Mister Skylock," the ship replied, and Rystar groaned.

"Got to fix that," she grumbled. "Come on, I'm sure they're waiting for us inside.

Shea and Enzo stood from their seats and followed her out of the door and towards the front steps of the Capitol, crouching in case any Horoths had survived the assault. When they encountered no resistance, they headed up the steps and were greeted by several Ya'ados, who held them at gunpoint. Rystar and her crew raised their arms and stopped at the top stair.

"We're here to see Ji'lan and his crew," Rystar announced, and the Ya'ados looked to each other before nodding and gesturing for them to follow. Inside they went, passing through the foyer and a slew of injured Ya'ados and Sustri. The Ya'ados led them upstairs and to an office at the far side of the hall, where she noticed Kyran, Cobalt, Na'gya, and Ji'lan all standing over a table with a large map.

Kyran looked up. When he saw Enzo, he bolted across the room and pulled him into a tight hug, burying his face in Enzo's hair. Rystar smiled, a tear forming in the corner of her eye despite herself. Kyran's eyes were shiny when he drew away and flicked them over to Rystar, who he also pulled into a hug.

"Thank you, Ry," he whispered. "I can't thank you enough."

"Of course," she breathed back, kissing his cheek and letting go. Kyran grasped Shea's hand and began to talk with him while Cobalt approached and pulled Enzo close with a firm grip on his hand.

"Vida," Cobalt greeted, a huge smile on his face.

"If I didn't know any better, Torlick," Enzo said, pulling in Cobalt for a hug, "I'd say you missed me."

"*Tsëh*," Cobalt grumbled against the side of Enzo's head. They let go and separated, migrating towards the table Ji'lan stood near.

"We lost Lo'varth," he announced, and Rystar hung her head. He was never up on her list of people she liked, but Lo'varth had been important to the cause, and it pained her to see Ji'lan torn up over it.

"Ji'lan, is something happening at the base?" Enzo asked, walking up to the table and setting his tablet down. Ji'lan's eyes went wide, and he sighed, turning around to face a window overlooking the destruction of the bubble.

"The Wings of Freedom base in Sluirossi is gone," he said, shaking his head. "But it is not worth crying over. We have a far larger base here on Chure. Thanks to your friends here."

He twisted to face them and threw Rystar a small smile before heading back to the table and setting a hand down on it. Enzo scrunched his brow and picked his tablet back up, swiping through it as he plopped down in a chair nearby. Rystar headed to the table and took in the map splayed out on it, lines and X's marking it all over.

"Is this Chure?" she asked.

"Yes, and this is us, here," Ji'lan said and pointed to the Capitol building near the western side of the bubble. The rest of the bubble was full of factories and old buildings, not much worth occupying. "With you wiping out most of the Horoth forces outside of the Capitol, I've already sent more soldiers out to secure the perimeter. There will be no way in for them now."

"How long do you think you can hold them off?" Rystar asked.

"Now that they have to funnel down the main street here, indefinitely," Ji'lan replied with a grin. "Some of our fighters are repairing the Horoth tanks and stealing their LASSOs now. I am sure we will be able to fend them off as long as we can."

"Well, I'm glad we could help," Rystar said and folded her arms. If she were honest, she had no idea what she was doing, and Ji'lan thanking her for her instrumental part in capturing Chure didn't sit right. She should have done more.

"Ji'lan," Enzo said, rising from his seat and heading towards the table. "I'm sorry to have to show you this, but there's traffic going to the Horoth government in Sluirossi concerning the lo-

# CATACLYSM

cation of the base from Lo'varth. It happened yesterday."

"You lie, show me," Ji'lan snapped, stomping over to where Enzo stood and reading his tablet over his shoulder. Enzo pointed to something on his tablet, and Ji'lan took it, his eyes whipping across the screen. His face fell, and his shoulders slumped as he read on until finally, he pushed the tablet back to Enzo, who he sighed, sitting down in a chair near the opposite wall.

"It doesn't matter now," he said, head in his hands. "He is dead and atoned for his sin. For all we know, he did us a favor."

Silence filled the room, and they mourned the loss of a comrade despite his betrayal. Rystar eventually cleared her throat and sat a hand on one hip before addressing Ji'lan. "Earlier you said we needed help to take over Sluirossi. Do you still need it?"

Ji'lan snorted and looked up at her and the crew. "As good as you all are, you will not be enough to take over Sluirossi. We will need extra firepower for that."

"Where do you suggest we get it?" Kyran said, stepping forward. "We have all these factories. We can start making weapons and vehicles again."

"Yes, but with no bodies to power those weapons and vehicles, they are useless," Ji'lan said. "No, we need a strong force to come in to assist us."

Silence fell again before Cobalt snorted, unfolding his arms and pushing off from the wall, pointing at Ji'lan. "You're not thinking of asking the Atrex?"

"I am," Ji'lan said, eyeing Cobalt with interest.

"Will they come to your aid?" Cobalt asked, folding his arms and raising an eyebrow. Rystar looked from him back to Ji'lan like a dangerous ping-pong match, taking drags from her Cortijet.

"We will see," Ji'lan said and stood up, addressing Kyran directly now. "I must ask for your aid again. As the Captain of the *Firehawk* and a Sustri with the ability to travel far from here, will you go on my behalf and ask the Atrex for their assistance in the takeover of Sluirossi?"

"They're going to ask what they get in return," Kyran said, raising an eyebrow.

Ji'lan's wicked grin brightened the room as he let out a laugh and turned to look out of the window. "Tell them, a Horoth president's head on a pike and all the uranium they could ask for."

## CHAPTER TWELVE_
RYSTAR UMARA : DSV FIREHAWK

The *Firehawk* sat in the Yimesotwa spaceport, filling up its gas tank and receiving a checkup, which usually took several hours.

They had left Ji'lan and his soldiers down in the Chure bubble, now fully under Ya'ados and Sustri control. Rystar stood in the shower, letting the hot water rinse over her like it hadn't done in far too long. Kyran and Shea had both hounded her the second she walked through her bedroom door, locking it behind her for good measure.

Sure, she loved having the attention of two incredibly attractive people, but there was only so much she could handle at once. First, she needed a long, hot shower to rinse off the events of the day. Second, she needed Lupe to make her some decent food. She hadn't eaten since breakfast, and her stomach was a terrifying pit of despair.

Third, she needed to talk to Enzo.

Rystar did feel a little bad about putting Na'gya off again but decided he still needed some space after the looks he gave her and Shea whenever they entered a room. She exited the shower and toweled off, running a brush through her hair and brushing her teeth before entering her bedroom and tossing the towel on the bed, rummaging around in her closet for some clothes to wear.

She finally settled on a black tank and a worn pair of jeans, a pair of black socks to finish off the classic *'let's get together in your room'* look. Sighing, she looked down at herself and felt a vague sense of dread about what Enzo really thought about when he looked at her but shook it off and crossed the room to her door.

When she opened it, she really shouldn't have been surprised to see Kyran standing directly in front of her, but she sighed anyway and leaned against the doorframe. "Do you really just stand here and wait for me to leave?"

"Got nothing else better to do," he said with a shrug, that stupid, smug smile on back in place.

"Aren't you, like, the Antuso?" she asked, tilting her head and trying her tongue at Sisyen.

"*Antsuo*, and the ship's being serviced, don't have anything to do just yet," he replied. "And anyway, I wanted to talk to you about Enzo."

"Funny, I was just going to go talk to him," she said, pulling her door closed and leaning against it.

"I want to be completely honest with you," Kyran said.

"I'm glad, I'd like that, too," Rystar chuckled.

"When Enzo was gone this past month, I realized how much he meant to me," Kyran explained, his smug demeanor fading. "I realized that maybe some of those feelings I had a long time ago didn't leave."

Rystar nodded and stuck her thumbs in her pockets, tilting her head and trying to pinpoint the exact feeling in her chest. She wasn't able to. "Have you told him?"

"I'm trying to give him some space. It's his first day back on the ship," he said.

Rystar hummed. "I suppose you're right."

"What were you going to talk to him about?" Kyran asked, folding his arms across his chest.

"Pretty much the same thing you were, I think," she snorted, pushing off the door and stepping until she and Kyran were a foot apart. "Unless you want to go talk to him together."

"Oh, honey, I don't think there will be a lot of talking," Kyran said with a delicious smirk and pushed some hair from her face. She swatted his hand away but grabbed it, weaving their fingers together.

"Be serious," she said, swinging their arms and looking up at him through her eyelashes. Kyran's face softened, and he sighed.

"Fine," he relented, "I'm sure he'll appreciate not one, but two confessions of attraction on his first day back."

"Double the fun, come on," Rystar said, letting his hand go and heading towards the elevators. "Do you know where he is?"

"Usually he's down in his room. Let's check there," Kyran said and entered the elevator, pressing the button to bring them to the bottommost floor. Rystar had never been down here and blinked in the dim light. They turned left and walked down the hall until they saw a door on the left. Kyran knocked, waiting a moment before it creaked open, and a sliver of Enzo's face appeared.

"Hey, you two, what's going on?" he asked, opening the door a little more. "Is everything okay?"

"Everything's great. We just wanted to come and see you," Kyran said, glancing at Rystar, who nodded her agreement. "Mind if we come in?"

"Please," Enzo said, opening the door fully and waving them inside. It was just as dark in Enzo's room as it was outside, and it took a full minute for her eyes to become accommodated. A bed sat to their left. To their right was a wall of servers and blinking lights and cables, computer screens and keyboards hooked up to some. In front of them was another door that Rystar assumed led to a bathroom.

The door shut behind them, and Enzo apologized, clearing off a stack of papers and cables that covered a couch before indicating they should sit. They did, albeit a little awkwardly, and watched as Enzo sat cross-legged on the floor below them and picked up a keyboard, going back to whatever it was he was doing.

"What are you up to?" Rystar asked when it had been silent for too long.

"Trying to find out where that Marsters guy went," Enzo said, his long black hair waving around his face. Rystar took a moment to study him, the rich, oak tones of his skin in the blue light, his amber eyes as bright as any of the computer screens in his room.

"Well, stop for a moment. We need to talk," Kyran said, slipping down to the floor and pulling Enzo's hand into his own. Enzo looked up at him and set his keyboard down, gazing into Kyran's eyes before flicking them up to Rystar.

"What about?" Enzo said, pushing some hair from his face and furrowing his brow.

"I can't imagine what you went through this past month, Enz," Kyran began, looking everywhere but Enzo's face. "And I'm not saying we had it worse, but I went through some tough times without you here."

"Kind of hard to not have someone security-minded on board," Enzo snorted, but Kyran held his hand tighter.

"I meant as my friend," Kyran explained, pulling both of Enzo's hands into his own. Enzo gulped and flicked his eyes between Rystar and Kyran. Rystar gazed down at the pair of them and didn't have a shred of jealousy anywhere in her body, just a sense of warmness tingling through her bones and a low heat somewhere near her belly.

"I missed you, too," Enzo said in a quiet voice, his eyes focused on their hands. "All of you. I couldn't stop thinking about where we left off." He cast his gaze to Rystar, whose cheeks reddened as she slid down to the floor as well, placing a hand on Enzo's knee. "And I couldn't stop thinking about what if I didn't get a chance to tell you how I felt, Ky."

Kyran smiled and pulled Enzo close, wrapping his arms around Enzo's neck and letting out a huge sigh. When he let go, Kyran put a kiss to the top of Enzo's forehead and moved away, placing Enzo's hands on Rystar's.

"So tell me," he purred, his red eyes smoldering dangerously, "where did you two leave off?"

Enzo lowered his head and smiled, white fangs gleaming in the computer light. He raised an eyebrow and glanced up at Rystar, who shuddered under his gaze. Leaning forward, she pulled him closer by his hands and placed a light kiss on his lips as Kyran's hand slid around to the small of her back.

"I'll let you two catch up," Kyran said, leaning forward to kiss Rystar on the cheek before standing up.

"Are you sure?" Rystar asked and looked up at him, hands still entwined with Enzo's. Kyran looked between the two of them with that same face she had earlier and could not put a finger on what it was. It was happy, loving, warm, and something else, and it made her chest melt.

"I'm sure," Kyran said and crossed the room to

Enzo's door, letting himself out and shutting it behind him.

There was only a moment of awkward silence before Enzo pulled her close, and she climbed into his lap, wrapping her legs around his waist and her arms around his shoulders. She kissed him deeper and moaned at his insistence. Rystar didn't want to play favorites, but Enzo's taste was intoxicating. The way he rolled their tongues together and slid his hands up her shirt, and clawed at her back made her fall apart at his touch.

With some effort, he lifted them both up and sat her on the couch, crawling over her body and kissing down her neck and chest. Thumbs rubbed at her nipples through her shirt, and she thrust her chest further into his grasp. She grabbed at the hem of his shirt and yanked it up, over his head, and onto the floor where it splayed across a keyboard.

Enzo smiled and talked to her in between kisses, his low voice sending her over the edge. "I never did thank you for saving me."

"This is thanks enough," she said, muffled from his lips.

"I'm glad we got to pick up where we left off," he said, kissing down her jawline and neck, sucking bruises, and making Rystar cry out. She dug her nails into his back, and he sucked in a breath, biting at her collarbone.

"I'm glad we did, too," she said against his shoulder, "you're amazing."

"Eh," Enzo said with a shrug, slowly kissing down her body until he reached the waistband of her jeans and unbuttoned them. He pulled down the zipper and hooked his fingers in the waist, pulling down and helping Rystar kick them off fully.

It was incredibly comforting, laying there with

Enzo in her underwear and shirt while his warm body pressed against her legs as he let his lips linger against her thighs and hips. The couch barely fit the both of them, and they squeezed together until Enzo pulled away for a moment and reached to the floor to grab his tablet.

"I should have seen that coming," Rystar chuckled to herself, legs still wrapped around his knees. He let out a laugh and shook his head, tapping a few times on the tablet surface until a faint wavering of notes floated through the air. Back on the couch, he curled around her again, putting their foreheads together and kissing her cheekbones.

"Is this Sustri music?" she asked after a moment, the instruments hanging in the air foreign to her.

"Old, a couple hundred years old," he said. "Never could get into the new music of today."

"I don't even know what human music sounded like a couple hundred years ago," she scoffed. "It's amazing you can hold onto your history like that."

"Considering our age, it's not too far in the past," Enzo said with a shrug and pulled her into another kiss. She moaned and writhed under his hands, making their way down her body and under her shirt to set her skin alight again.

He lifted her up and sat back on the couch, settling her in his lap and grasping at her thighs, digging his fingers into the soft flesh there. Since coming on board the *Firehawk*, Rystar had become infinitely more okay with how she looked, considering what it did to her fellow crewmates. Any curve or roll she had, they grabbed. Any stretch mark or blemish, they kissed.

Enzo's hands slid under her shirt again and pulled it over her head, tossing it on the floor away from the computers. Rystar chuckled. At least someone on board was just as much of an animal as she was. With a hand on the back of her neck, he pulled her down and into a kiss, and she pushed her hips down in his lap. His mouth opened against hers, and she took the opportunity to dive her tongue in and taste him.

He was hands and cobber fiber and the computer screens cast a blueish glow on his face as he looked up at her, glowing amber eyes piercing through her soul. They almost seemed on fire until he closed them while she pushed down in his lap again, and he grabbed at his jeans like they burned him.

She sat up to allow him room to yank them off and toss them elsewhere. He took her hand in his and pulled her down again, this time with nothing separating the two of them except for the thin strip of cloth that she refused to take off just yet.

Enzo was huge and she pressed herself down on him, the warmness radiating from her core enveloping him as she spun slowly in circles, hitting her spot with each turn. Throwing her head back, she sent her hands splaying on his chest and dug in as hard as his were on her thighs, circling faster. Rystar's hips swayed erratically. Her mouth dropped open as the familiar burn coursed through her lower back and upper thighs. Enzo rubbed them and pulled her face down for another kiss.

"Come for me now," he whispered against her lips, and she exploded, letting out a soft cry and pressing their foreheads together as she fell apart in his arms.

They sat there for a moment while Rystar caught her breath, and she shook her head to get rid of some strands of hair. She eyed him and raised her eyebrows for a second while a smug grin appeared on her face, and she moved down to kneel between his legs.

"Your turn," she breathed and sank down on him in one go, tasting herself on him and moaning. He let out a soft groan as the back of her throat hit his head, and he tangled a hand in her hair, squeezing gently. She pulled up and swirled her tongue around him, coming up for air and turning her eyes to gaze at him through her eyelashes.

"*Sipe*, Ry," he sighed as she dropped again, hollowing her cheeks and sliding along his length. He hissed between his teeth as she continued, and his other hand found her shoulder, leaning forward to pull her arm up so he could entwine their fingers together.

Rystar picked up the pace, wrapped her free hand around his base, pumping in time with her mouth, and twisting her legs together. She longed for him but continued, moaning as he stiffened harder in her mouth and his legs shook around her. His hand squeezed hers tighter, and she sunk down one last time until he hit the back of her throat again and released with a cry.

He twitched in her mouth, and she finally released him, still gripping the base with her fist while she licked his tip to clean it off. He shuddered, watching her every move with his cat-like eyes. Enzo let his head tip back against the couch and caught his breath, broad chest wavering up and down in the low light.

She eventually climbed up on top of him and nestled in the crook of his arm, and he wrapped it around her, twirling her hair with his fingers.

"Was that thanks enough?" he muttered, brow furrowing. "Seems like I had a much better time than you did."

"Oh, hush," she scoffed, swatting at his chest. He

laughed and pulled her closer, kissing the top of her head and sighing.

After a moment, she twisted her head to rest her chin on his chest and frowned. "What did you tell the Horoths that made Kyran trust them?"

"Hm?" Enzo hummed, pulling himself out of a doze. He thought for a moment before sniffing. "I told them, 'if you were strong enough to survive his death, you could go on long enough to live like he wanted you to.'"

Rystar thought on that for a moment, turning her head to rest her cheek on his chest again and wondering just how much her grandfather meant to Kyran.

They must have fallen asleep like that because the sound of Rystar's tablet ringing made them both jump. She scurried down off the couch to grab it and saw Kyran on the other line.

"Sorry to bother you lovebirds, but ship's almost done," he crooned. "If you can find the time, will you join us on the bridge?"

"Of course we will. Don't be like that," she huffed, sitting back on her haunches and scrolling through her missed messages.

"Not being like anything, sugar, just want to make sure you have enough time to… talk," he said with that smug voice of his.

"Go away. We'll be there soon," she said and swiped the call closed.

"We're not leaving tonight, are we?" Enzo asked, pulling his jeans and shirt back on while Rystar did the same.

"We shouldn't be. I think he just wants to talk plans for our next move," she said with a shrug, pulling her socks on.

They stood up, and Rystar made to head to the

door, but Enzo caught her hand and pulled her to him. Pushing a strand of hair from her face and letting a thumb stroke her cheek, he smiled at her through a curtain of black hair.

"I'm glad you came to talk to me," he said in a low voice. "I was starting to think you weren't interested."

"I've been interested for a long time," she admitted, bringing her arms up to rest on his shoulders. "This just isn't something I've done before. Try to be with more than one person at once, much less all of you."

"We're a handful, no doubt," he chuckled and kissed her forehead. Enzo was shaping up to be the sweetest person she had ever been with, his words, the way he stroked her skin so delicately, the soft kisses he placed wherever he could. She smiled and narrowed her eyes as if the sting of tears were there but took in a deep breath instead and kissed him on the cheek.

"Come on, let's figure out our next move," she said, heading towards the door with him in tow.

---

She could have sworn Shea gave her a quick, genuine smile when she and Enzo walked through the door together. It seemed as if Shea was her personal cheerleader now, the way he pushed her to be with the rest of the crew. Na'gya, on the other hand, looked less than pleased, and a surge of guilt shot through her. She was supposed to talk to him, too.

"So, Painger," Kyran said and clapped his hands together, winking at Enzo, who flushed. "Lupe, what can you tell us about Painger."

"Lava world," Lupe said, swiveling around in their

chair. "Full of rocks and mountains. Don't know why you keep taking us to these shitty places." They grinned and tapped their nose at Rystar, who chuckled but stopped when Kryan threw her a deadly look.

"Because that's the closest planet of the Atrex," he explained and stepped down to the console to bring up a map of several Atrex systems. The closest was Sesbawg, full of other rocks and lava worlds they had no business being on. "The Sesbawg system has Painger, which has the third to largest military force of Atrex."

"Why not go to Pawydezis?" Enzo asked, nose buried in his tablet.

"I don't want to bother the capital with this just yet," Kyran said, waving him off. "Besides, the Me'ebawg system—" he pointed to a system just past the Sesbawg one where they were headed "—is about 8 jumps away. We'd need to stop at Painger anyway for another gas up."

"And food," Rystar grumbled, her stomach doing the same.

"The Atrex have a diet more similar to yours," Lupe said.

"Thank goodness," Rystar said and rolled her eyes.

Kyran studied the map more with Lupe, and Rystar meandered over to Enzo as Shea approached them both.

"And how are you two?" he asked, a knowing grin on his face.

"We're doing just fine," Rystar said, plopping down next to Enzo and reading his tablet over his shoulder. "In fact, I was coming over here to ask you something serious. Did you find out anything about Marsters?"

"He covers his tracks pretty well," Enzo said as Shea sat down on his other side, furrowing his brow and playing with his lip ring. "He was definitely able to track you down when you pinged out to the Galactic Internetwork, but beyond that, he goes ghost. The FDDS must have some badass systems."

"They're nothing to shake a stick at," Rystar said, chewing a knuckle and pulling out her Cortijet. "Do you think he'll follow us to Painger?"

"I think now that he knows our signatures and has access to FDDS resources, like border gate information," Enzo said, raising his eyebrows at her, "he will certainly be able to find us wherever we go."

Rystar stared out of the space shield at Yimesotwa's sun, some name she couldn't pronounce but held meaning to the Sustri people. There wasn't much in the universe that could scare her, but a madman hellbent on taking her crew down and had the entirety of the FDDS's resources at his disposal?

Terrifying.

## ABOUT THE AUTHOR_

At the age of five, Jack published their first book, "My Lost Cat", and it all went downhill from there. Jack has splattered pages across the writing genre spectrum, from post-rock songs to short stories, fanfiction to legislative policies. In 2012, they finally settled down for seven years and penned the first of the Homestead Trilogy, "Florida is Gone", based on the apocalypse predictions of the same year.

Jack is working as a cyber security architect and raises a son with their two husbands in the middle of a Florida swamp. In between taking their son to explore the corners of the state and working, Jack finds time to write as much as they can and hopes to one day leave the technical life behind to live a life in a swampy, solitary fantasy world. Until then, they'll stick with their day job.

facebook.com/jackarcherauthorgroup
twitter.com/jackfromflorida
instagram.com/jack_from_florida

ALSO BY JACK ARCHER_

Firehawk: Rystar and the LASSOS Book One
Krimson Princess: Rystar and the LASSOs Book Two
Florida is Gone
The Government is Gone
Futeuropa
Beautiful Apocalypse
Beguiling Beasts
Love Sucks

Made in the USA
Columbia, SC
23 May 2022